LOVELAND PUBLIC LIBRARY

000636627

8/31/21
$14.95
9/21

Havana Hallelujah

WITHDRAWN

D1528290

Havana Hallelujah

A NOVEL

DAVID SMITH-SOTO

Copyright © 2020 David Smith
All rights reserved

The characters and events portrayed in this book are fictitious.
Any similarity to real persons, living or dead, is coincidental
and not intended by the author.

No part of this book may be reproduced, or stored in a
retrieval system, or transmitted in any form or by any means,
electronic, mechanical, photocopying, recording, or otherwise,
without express written permission of the author.
Contact: OldCamera@me.com

ISBN: 979-8-5672-4025-0

INDEPENDENTLY PUBLISHED

COVER AND BOOK DESIGN: ROGER FIDLER

This book also is available as a Kindle e-book from Amazon.com.

For Zita

Where is the wisdom we have lost in knowledge?
Where is the knowledge we have lost in information?

THE ROCK — T.S. ELIOT, 1934

Contents

Foreword

David Smith-Soto's novel Havana Hallelujah is a complex and richly drawn portrait of the peoples and landscapes of the Americas, of the lies and machinations of politicians and spies, of the dangerous jobs journalists must face each day trying to separate facts from lies and propaganda.

Havana Hallelujah is a fascinating and remarkably complex psychological exploration of Jonas Harding's traumas and those of the many characters he meets along the way — a novel that stays with us long after we've read it.

In the novel, we follow Harding, a Costa-Rican-born American journalist and photographer, as he chases stories from Virginia to Miami, from Guatemala City to Havana, first trying to discover why no one can find a dignified burial place for a homeless black man in the Deep South, then, working for a Miami newspaper, trying to discover who ordered a village massacre at Salta Tigre, Cubans infiltrating Guatemala or the Guatemalan Army itself.

The reporter is caught up in the assassination of the Guatemalan Army Chief of Staff in a jungle firefight, then in the shooting of a security agent for the Guatemalan President while attending a service at the Miami Church of Family Reunification. All this amid terrorist attacks and the mass exodus of Cuban boat people searching for freedom in the U.S.

LEX WILLIFORD, AUTHOR OF MACAULEY'S THUMB
AND SUPERMAN ON THE ROOF

Williford's novella, Balsa and Tissue Paper, is a selection in both a Ploughshares Solos longform issue and as a single e-book; his other books have won the 1993 Iowa Short Fiction Award and the 2016 Rose Metal Flash Fiction chapbook award. Former bilingual MFA program chair, he teaches at UT, El Paso.

Loveland Public Library
Loveland, CO

CHAPTER ONE

Nowhere Man

He's a real nowhere Man,
Sitting in his Nowhere Land
— JOHN LENNON AND PAUL MCCARTNEY

Halfman

I was right on the ambulance's tail as it wailed to a stop like a red hearse with a cherry on top. As I pulled up, a sheet of paper fluttered out of my open Jeep and I caught Goldy's eye and knew he had spotted the flying scrap. He hated litter worse than anything and had already cited me for stuff flying out of the Jeep. He looked at me like I was littering his highway just to piss him off. Two paramedics jumped out and started working on one man. Goldy ignored a second guy stretched out on his side, sort of resting his head on one forearm, dead.

Deputy Sheriff Goldy Goldebrand glanced at me like he had decided not to mention the scrap of paper because I was hopeless, and he looked at the tires of the dust-covered green International pickup resting on its crushed top in a gulley by the side of the road.

"Bald as my goddamn head," he said. He passed his hand over a tire, pulled off his hat and wiped his forehead with his sleeve. "Where the hell's the other wagon?"

"Right behind us, Goldy," the paramedic said, pulling on the last strap. "We're out of here, man."

I aimed the Nikon and squeezed off two shots of the gurney slamming into the ambulance, one of Goldy's bald pate, and then focused on the dead man, careful to keep the wrecked pickup in the background. Right there through the viewfinder, it came to me, maybe because I was looking with the bad eye. It was like Nam. I didn't feel shit, just looking for the money shot.

The numbness worried me. I thought I was leaving it behind, and I thought about it later too, but at that moment, I was more worried about Goldy hating litter.

Goldy had the tape out, measuring the skid marks. There were no signs of another car. "What do you make of it, Goldy?" He answered like each word cost him money, and he glanced over at me after every few words just to measure my reaction.

"Single-car accident, bald tires, skidded on the shoulder, flipped… gravity." He spit a neat little package at the Jeep. "Like that deathtrap you're driving, high center of gravity." Then I saw Bernie waving and yelling from a gulley a hundred yards behind the wreck.

"Another one over here."

Goldy looked at the dirt and pulled his hat off again shaking his head and gave me that litter-hating look. I just chased my motorized Nikon up the blacktop and let it whirr.

———

I wiped a bubble off a wet photo and held it up to the safelight, rubbing the developer into the shadows to darken them up a little. Good blacks, good grays, just enough white. With the lights on, only the outline of the third man's body showed in the foreground, and then the sloping hill of wild grass rolling down to the bridge as Route 7 forms a horseshoe just before crossing the Shenandoah.

I remembered the first time I saw that view, the year before, as my Jeep crested the Blue Ridge, the glinting Shenandoah river below me and Ashby, Virginia. Way beyond in the valley, about a hundred miles and a hundred years away from Washington, D.C., the University of Maryland and the war. Looking at the valley then, I felt like an alien from another dimension altogether, appraising it from a distant and obscured place, from beyond America, even beyond Vietnam. I was just starting to see well enough to shoot the Nikons again and hear clearly and more than that, I was just learning to think again for myself. A year before, the doc at the hospital in San Diego told me I had a rice paddy in my left eye.

"Look, Harding, we just stapled the back of the inside of your eye back into place — the retina, the part that sees. It'll take some time to come back. Whatever hit you slammed your eye like a meteor hitting a rice paddy spreading rice shoots flat all around the point of impact. Those shoots have to stand back up before you can see well out of that eye." Sitting there one-eyed and ears ringing, I just said, "shit, fucking rice shoots."

"Look at it this way, Private. You could have lost the eye and half your face. I've seen that."

"What about the ringing in my head?"

"That'll be there. One day you'll wonder where it went."

Just as I placed my timorous footprints on the mall at the university, Neil Armstrong took a lunar step for mankind. But for me, Maryland was more distant than the moon, hard to see and hard to hear. I had a year to go, and I was timorous. I started to relearn words like timorous. That year, students protesting the Vietnam War barricaded US-1 in front of the university, tried to burn down the armory and tear gas rolled down the lawns. I didn't give a shit. I'd already been given my share of the war, and I focused only on graduating and moving on. Slowly, my eye healed and my sense of self began to reappear west of the Blue Ridge after Bart Marvin answered my résumé. The Ashby Morning Sun had an opening for a photo halfman.

———

"What the hell is that?" I said, shifting in the black leather armchair in the lounge at the Ashby Country Club, dark as a funeral parlor. Bart laughed.

"I need a photographer, and I need a police reporter, and I've only got enough money for one man. At twenty-five you're older than I was when I started, but the governor is partial to vets, Purple Heart, too."

"I wasn't there long, just enough to get my head bashed in."

An older black man in a white jacket appeared, his round face smiling.

"Bourbon?" Bart said.

"Jack Daniel's on the rocks," I said.

Bart winked at the waiter. "Virginia Gentleman all around, Albert. It's a private club, Jonas. You still can't buy liquor by the drink in Ashby County, so members keep a bottle here at the club."

"Bourbon's all right."

"And you can write. That's a plus. Didn't know the Army taught that in basic."

"Taught me how to shoot the M-16 and the Nikons. I learned the writing at Maryland. Didn't know it was for newspapers, though. Never even read papers, until now, of course."

"Me, too," Bart laughed again, downed the bourbon and waved for another. "But it grows on you. What do you think of the club, Jonas? See those columns outside? Porch of the old courthouse. Freemont burned it down before Stonewall whipped his ass, but these columns were saved for a hundred years and we restored them and put them up again when we built this place, real Corinthians. See the filigree?"

"So what?"

"There's only two kind of columns in the Valley, Doric and Ionic. You'll see them in the old places. Dorics came first, square tablets on top, austere, usually with Hessian stonework, then the Ionics, scrolled tops rounded like a woman's lips, but these" — he took a deep breath — "are ecstatic, carved in Florence. They're the only ones. We built the club around them."

———

I left the prints of the Route 7 wreck on the engraver's light table and hurried to the newsroom to write the story. I was tired, but I could almost hear Bart telling me, "write it now even though you're beat. Tomorrow you'll forget the best stuff." Bart liked to teach, and I was learning. Three takes by mid-night. Who's the man?

The Sun held a centric corner in downtown Ashby separated from the county courthouse by a small park of patchy grass, a few black-olive trees, some cement benches, and a Confederate soldier standing guard. Up one street and you hit the courthouse; up the other and you were in Mount Zion Cemetery. I could see the funerals go by from my desk.

One time, just as Mr. Weaver leaned over me, breathing his gentle halitosis, asking for the caption to the front-page color photo, a crazed steer thundered past the newsroom's open door, cops chasing it. I grabbed the Nikon and bounded through the door, spotting them just as they disappeared past the gates into the expansive rolling grass of Mount Zion Cemetery. I ran to catch up and breathless, with my camera cocked, I peered around the headstones and mausoleums, finding only bucolic silence. Then a rushing crescendo and the steer kicked up sod as it bolted toward me, but as if yanked by an invisible halter, it froze right in front of General Turner Ashby's grave, staring hangdog. It was quiet all around, just the animal's snorting. They tied chains around the steer, foam dripping from its throbbing snout, and hooked the links to a pickup, but the animal wouldn't budge. Finally, aiming carefully, Goldy shot it point-blank near the ear with his thirty-eight. Blood poured out, but the animal wouldn't die. Goldy had to shoot it three times before it collapsed. I got a good shot of Goldy executing the steer. You could read Ashby's tombstone in the wet print. He had been promoted to general, but never got his star. He was killed at Good's Farm down by Harrisonburg two weeks later.

Nowhere Land

The sheriff's office and the jail were in the basement of the courthouse. Goldy's shift was over, and Bernie was the dispatcher on duty. Still wearing his trooper's hat, Bernie looked a lot like Goldy, well over six feet and 250 pounds, easy. It was a Hessian look, I found out from Bart. He was big on history. The Hessian mercenaries of the Revolutionary War had settled this part of Virginia, had built a lot of stone walls, and their offspring grew tall and stout in the Shenandoah Valley. The photos and the initial accident story were in the newspaper; now I needed details for the next day's follow-up. Bernie spoke in a slow, steady drawl without letting go of the fat mike, looking like he was broadcasting on NBC radio, circa 1932, reading a script instead of the police blotter.

"Well, you know two were DOA at Ashby Memorial," Bernie said.

"Yep. Did you confirm all the IDs?" I said.

"Johnny Perry, nineteen, from over in Bush County, DOA, and John McIntyre, also nineteen of Ashby in critical condition, in a coma. The other DOA was a John Doe. Looks like the Perry boy was driving. No seat belts of course."

"Bernie, I already wrote that story. What's new?" I'd probably have to write the obits. "Any funeral arrangements?"

"Yeah, actually the DOAs are already over at Fitzgerald's Funeral Home. They'll give you the details."

"What do you know about the John Doe?"

"Looks like he was on foot, near where the horseshoe turn dips, slopes down to the river. The International spots him too late, skids, and hits him. Then loses control, tries to regain and flips. We put out a bulletin and fingerprints, but hang on —" Bernie turned the page. The new stuff was always last. "This just came back from Baltimore. Not a John Doe anymore — Jimmy Wilson, homeless guy from Towson, Maryland, last known address a shelter near Baltimore. No family, no home, no history. Nobody."

"Any toxicology report?"

"No mention. Check with Memorial." The radio blared and Bernie tilted his hat at the mike, blocking his face from my view. That was it for him. Talking to Bernie reminded me of the Army's businesslike discourse about the dead. Enough of that kind of talk and you kind of die too, and then it's hard to summon the strength to come back to life.

If the DOAs were already at Fitzgerald's then there was no autopsy. Bob Fitzgerald was the deputy mayor of Ashby. I had photographed him that week announcing a proposal to issue bonds to pay for the downtown revitalization program. "We'll close Main Street, make it a pedestrian mall," Fitzgerald told The Sun. "No traffic, just shoppers, shops and clean air." The door to the funeral home's waiting room was unlocked.

"Hey, Bob, you home?"

Cissy Mae Fitzgerald, the deputy mayor's wife stepped into the foyer. A slender fortyish woman in equestrian costume with white lace curled at her throat thrust her hand at me with a wrestler's grip. She pulled off her helmet and dropped it and a short whip on the sofa. Her blond pageboy cut whirled as she freed herself from the helmet.

"Hi Jonas. I'm Cissy. We met at the board meeting on the downtown plan." She talked with the emphasis of having just chased a fox on horseback.

"Sure. I remember, City Planner."

Fitzgerald appeared at the door in a spotted white apron that came right up to the polka dots on the tight Windsor of his blue necktie. He wrung a towel in his hands. "Well, if it isn't Sir Jonas Harding, defender of the Fourth Estate."

"Hey, Bob. I'm covering that accident on Route 7. Two dead. Bernie says they're already here."

"Yep. Well, one of them anyway."

"You know if there was a toxicology report?"

"None of my concern. But I can tell you, off the record, the Perry boy smells like a still. Embalmed in bond. Funeral scheduled for Saturday at Mount Zion Cemetery."

"And the other guy?"

"Don't know. Wouldn't embalm him anyway. With no next of kin claiming him, he was going into Potter's Field, back section of Zion."

"Who pays for that?"

"City would."

"That why they're here right away?"

"Hey, Jonas, what you driving at? You mean, they were sent right to the deputy mayor's funeral home? Well, we have a contract with the city for the John Does. Sealed bids. All done right. The other guy's not here anyway."

"Where is the other guy?"

"He's over at Quincy's barbershop."

"Barbershop?"

"Sure. Quincy Brown keeps a funeral parlor in the back for colored."

"You mean, they brought him here and you sent him along to Quincy?"

"Sure. Lookit, contract states that we get all the John Does and bury them in Potter's Field at Zion. But no colored. There's no colored in Zion. They should've sent him right over to Quincy, waste of time. So I subcontracted him out to Quincy."

"Not even in Potter's Field?"

"Nope. Not even in Potter's Field."

"What about Jews?"

Fitzgerald paused a moment knowing I was being a smart ass, and I was, but he knew he'd better give me a straight answer in case he had to read it in tomorrow's Sun. "Long's they're not colored Jews."

Beauty quote, I thought. "So, where they going to bury him?"

"Funny thing. I've had that contract with the city for years, and I never got a colored John Doe before. It would have to be the colored cemetery. Talk to Quincy about it."

"So, you don't handle any funerals for colored?"

"No. Not that we have that many dead colored in Ashby now anyway, small community. Quincy does them, and the burials are over at Delaney's on the east side, down by the river. Nice view."

It was raining now. Gray gusts and clapping thunder swept me into the barbershop. Quincy Brown and his family lived on top and Quincy ran his funeral home in the back. A few black men lingered, waiting for the rain to stop. The window air conditioner shot cold air into the room. Little blue ribbons on the vents fluttered at Quincy, the way they do at Sears.

"Yes, he's here," Quincy said. He was rotund, but he moved gracefully, snapping the scissors in quick delicate cuts as he worked on a customer.

"Well, what about the funeral?" I asked.

"Won't be a funeral, the way we usually do a funeral."

"Why not? I thought he'd go to Potter's Field at Delaney."

"Well, there's no Potter's Field at Delaney."

"So, what do you do?"

"Don't rightly know yet. Haven't had a colored John Doe in years."

"Quincy, it's really hard to understand that."

"I know, but it's true. Think about it. You're a colored man from somewhere else, maybe D.C. You don't have any business in Ashby, Virginia. Colored don't have any business in Ashby."

"But he's got to get buried, doesn't he? Why can't you just bury him at Delaney?"

Quincy stopped cutting and looked around the barbershop, at the green walls and at the black and chrome recliners. "Look, you're not from around here," he said, enveloping me with his eyes, steadily, kindly. "There's no more room at Delaney. Hasn't been any room for years. All the spots are taken. My family has two left. One is mine; the other's for my wife."

"He could be cremated and put in a little box. Wouldn't take up much space. Or just scattered on the Shenandoah."

"Too late for that. The city has to pay Fitzgerald for the delivery and pay me for the funeral and probably pay me to embalm him since it's going to be a while and he'd have to go clear to Roanoke for cremation and then what? Back here?"

I yanked the Jeep's flimsy door shut. Water leaked through the top, settling on the dashboard. I looked at the barbershop with my bad eye. It looked all twisted and screwed up. I looked at it with my good eye. It looked like a good old barbershop. Everything has two aspects, I thought, and one of them is all screwed up. I closed both eyes and leaned on the steering wheel, resting there, putting the story together in my mind, the rain pattering on the Jeep. I drove back to The Sun and as I finished writing, feeling tired and irritable, longing for a quick Jack Daniel's, I wondered about my place in this Southern town somehow stuck in the 1950s.

"Nice shots."

I looked up from the Underwood and stared at Clarke Bowden for a moment, still thinking about the embalming room in the back of Quincy's barbershop.

"Nice shots," she said again, louder. "The accident on Route 7."

Clarke was an Ashby native. A slim woman, thirties but looking twenties, always in blue jeans and always rushing, straight blond hair pulled back, camera in hand. She was The Sun's full-time photographer. The rest of the newsroom staff usually just ignored me, but photography brought us together. I liked her no-bullshit manner, the intense blue eyes, the finely shaped nose and the harsh masculine name they give rich Southern girls. I thought about her, but she was married to an internist at Ashby Memorial.

"Thanks. Working on the follow-up now."

"Well, I heard on the radio that the McIntyre boy was hanging on, looks like he'll live. I know his parents."

"Yeah, but no, no, that's not the story. Those boys hit a black guy on Route 7, killed him. And he can't get buried. Bob Fitzgerald won't touch him even if it's good city money paying for the burial because the guy is black and anyway they don't plant colored people in Zion, anywhere in Zion. So Bob sends the corpse over to Quincy Brown's barbershop."

"Yes, I know he's the colored undertaker around here."

"But hang on. Quincy won't bury him anywhere either. There's no more room over in the colored cemetery, and it can't expand. The river's on one side, and the county sewage treatment plant's on the other. Jimmy Wilson is still homeless."

"No shit."

———

I parked the dirty gray Jeep on the street a hundred yards away from the Corinthian columns of the Ashby Country Club. I could have driven up the long circular driveway, but I wanted to walk on the grass and think a minute before meeting Bart.

The governor had called, and it wasn't the governor's style to get involved in a story, Bart said. He owned the newspaper, but he never forgot their agreement: Bart ran the newspaper. Once in a while, though, he would call, make a suggestion, and ask for an editorial, usually on an economic or a tax issue. This time he just wanted to chat about the Jimmy Wilson story a bit, Bart said. It was interesting. A traffic accident, normally a two-incher on the local page, wouldn't go away. It seemed there was a new angle every day, going on now for three weeks. And they all had a Jonas Harding byline.

As I recalled what Bart said, I wished I could forget about Jimmy Wilson. With each day, each story, Jimmy got closer to a resting place, then another hitch and Jimmy was back in the barbershop. Anonymous letters started to come in, usually threatening that shithead from Maryland. One of them found out I was Costa Rican-born and his request was "go back to that shithole country you came from." It was Vietnam again. Clarke made me think back about the war one day over a beer. "Are you against the war now?" she asked. "I don't know," I said. "It's not my war now." But I still had the anger. While I was gathering the facts for the stories, I didn't think about feelings, but there in front of the Corinthians I felt a slow seething anger and I didn't like it. That anger was unpredictable. It could take me anywhere. It was the old Vietnam anger, helpless anger at gratuitous, faceless death, and Jimmy Wilson was like that, a strengthening vortex sucking me in. Ashby was sick of the story, somehow threatened by the story, and I couldn't do a damn thing about anything. Just try to stay alive. Don't get caught up in the shit. It can kill you. But the story wouldn't die.

I waited in the cool dark lounge of the club for Albert to bring me some of Bart's Virginia Gentleman.

"You know anything about the governor, anything about recent Virginia history?" Bart said.

"Not much. I'm a Maryland boy."

"The governor was elected in the late fifties to preserve segregation in Virginia. And he tried, fought against any change. They all did, the old-guard Southerners, but when the time came, he obeyed the law of the land. He carried the state across that divide."

"That why so many colored leave Ashby?"

Bart ignored the barb and went on, "D.C.'s always been a strong draw for the young —"

"What'd he say about Jimmy Wilson?"

"Well that's not his style, to be direct like that." When he talked about the governor Bart always mentioned the governor's style. "He thought about it and then he said what he always says at first, 'It's an interesting situation.'"

"That's all?"

"No. He also said, 'that Harding boy's a good reporter.' He admires that. The Sun's been in his family since 1892 and he understands journalism and its privileged place in a community. Then, all he said was, 'I'd keep a good reporter on a good story.'"

"Jesus, Bart, I'm tired of the fucking story. I'm tired of Jimmy riding on my back, day after day, for weeks. Why's this story sticking to me? Who said I had to carry him?"

"Luck of the draw, my boy, and anyway, it turned out you had a good strong back. But the story is getting heavy all around, advertisers starting to complain. Look, just think of this story as a little dark cloud floating over Ashby, no, a bird, one of those little ducks. Ever hunt ducks?"

"Can't shoot ducks with an M-16, just people."

"Yep, need a shotgun. One of those smooth English beauties and you lead the ducks, can't shoot straight at them. Harlequin ducks, painted dark on top and white spots underneath that make it down to the Chesapeake and then flap away back up north as the season changes. Hey, anyway, soon as it's scheduled, I'd like you to drive down to Richmond and cover the hearing on the downtown revitalization bond issue. And while you're there, stop by The News Leader and talk to Jerry Penn, the ME. There's an opening for a reporter over there, and I talked to him about you. Bigger paper, check it out. He's interested."

I caught my breath, and I looked at him through the bad eye. No, Bart wouldn't be devious. He'd kick my ass all the way to Richmond if he wanted to fire me. Right there, I realized I'd gotten attached, attached to the old massive wooden desks in The Sun newsroom, the smell of ink that wafted in from the pressroom, the clatter of the Underwoods, the AP Teletype machine that never stopped banging and old Mr. Weaver yelling "copy, for Chrissake, copy!" as he rode the afternoon deadline. As it turned out, that meeting was postponed and I never met the Managing Editor of the Richmond News Leader.

"I guess I'm ready to graduate, move up from halfman, eh?"

Albert placed the chilled glass smartly, soundly, on the mahogany table as if he were dovetailing it into the wood. "Jack Daniel's on the rocks for Mr. Harding," he said.

For an instant, Bart caught the waiter's eye. "You already graduated," he said.

———

I found out the governor sat on the board of directors of Zion Cemetery, but I avoided focusing on that point. Jimmy was already opening a lot of old wounds, and I didn't see any point in upsetting the old man. He was partial to one-eyed vets. Jimmy was getting heavier every day, and each day something else popped up. Nothing serious. It was timid, gentle unrest, but Ashby had never seen much turmoil before, even in the sixties during the height of the racial protests in the rest of the country, so it drew attention. Colored girls were protesting publicly at Ashby High because they didn't make the cheer-leading team and only one colored kid qualified for varsity football, second string at that. A colored couple pitched a tent in front of the new development on Valley Avenue and said they wouldn't move until they could rent one of the empty apartments. Clarke caught a shot of sheriff's deputies pushing demonstrators off the Ashby High School green. One black girl gave her the finger. Clarke caught that too just before a deputy shoved the girl to the ground, holding her down with a boot close to her face. That was Clarke's last frame on that roll. Mr. Weaver played the finger shot on the front, caused quite a stir.

The money shot

"So, who's shooting the big game tonight?" It was Clarke.

I knew she wanted to avoid the hassle of shooting the color.

"I'll do the color for the front page, and you cover with black and white for Sports. When you going to do the color?"

"Never. I love black and white."

Doing color for the front page was an arduous task, but I loved the precision of the process. You had to be careful. A few extra dots on the printing plate and the color went to muddy hell. I would shoot the first quarter with the big color camera and get back to the paper to develop the slides and print the color separations. I'd be done by two a.m., easy.

Standing on the twenty-yard line, I gazed coolly at the screaming fans in the bleachers and at the players. I didn't know which team was which and didn't care. I was only waiting for the money shot. The Hasselblad had twelve shots, but I only needed one good one and it was back to the peace of the darkroom in the basement of The Sun. It was a clumsy camera for sports, more like handling a grenade launcher than a rifle, but I needed the large image for the color separations.

The ball was at mid-field. The quarterback called the play and handed the ball to the running back just as the viewfinder framed him turning the corner, rushing toward me like a crazed steer I once knew. I led him steadily through the lens, timing the shot so I could step back as he broke a tackle and filled the frame. I squeezed the trigger. The camera mirror flipped up, blacking out the viewfinder, and just as I stepped back, squarely, surely, just as I'd planned, a sudden shove pushed me right back into the rusher's path and he knocked me flying into the players' bench. I looked up at faces and tried to sit up but couldn't breathe. I turned over spitting dirt and gasping for air and lay there like a choking baby until my lungs started to work and then managed to sit up. I was blind until I realized my contact lenses had shifted. I closed my eyes and pushed them back into place. I opened the good eye. It still worked. I checked the bad eye, still fucked up, but no worse. Someone handed me the Hasselblad. The lens was muddy, but the back had held and the film was safe. I saw Clarke twisting toward me.

"Jonas, let me help you." She grabbed the camera bag and the equipment as I staggered to the Jeep. "I think we should go to Ashby Memorial and get you checked out."

17

"No, I'm ok," I paused, gasping. Now the ribs started to hurt, but I felt around and knew there was no real break. "Shoot the rest of the game. I'm going back to The Sun. The film's OK." I leaned on the car, shaking. "No. I'm going with you," she said.

Clarke slid behind the steering wheel of the Jeep and burned the tires speeding out of the stadium, onto Route 50 heading back to Ashby, glancing at me now and then. My neck ached now, and I leaned my head on the side window, eyes closed.

"Somebody shoved me," I said, trying to catch my breath. "I had the shot timed perfectly, and some sonofabitch pushed me." She didn't say it, but she had a shot of me flying into the bench, the crowd scampering, arms in the air.

"I really think we should go to the emergency room."

"No, I'm going to finish the color."

"You're kidding."

"No. I'm not kidding. That color will be on tomorrow's front page."

"I'll help you."

We developed the film slowly, mechanically, my arms still trembling. It was a seven-step process, and in between the steps, exhausted, she accidentally opened the tank in the light. We both rushed to slam the lid back on, and she looked at me terrified. Then she began crying helplessly.

"It's ok, at that point it won't fog."

"It's not that," she said. And then I hugged her. "It's not that," I said, crying too and felt her sobs sink into my chest. She looked up at me, and I kissed her eyes. I kissed her mouth. She didn't pull back. I kneeled on the cold tiled floor of the darkroom and pulled her down. She came to me and held tight. When I kissed her breasts through the blouse, she said, "Don't. Not here."

We finished the work, and Clarke left, placing the color separations on the engraver's light-table. I leaned back in the swivel chair in the comfort of the darkened newsroom, and I knew a new stage of life in Ashby had started. Again, the hill of wild grass sloped down to the Shenandoah, and when I opened my eyes to Bart Marvin leaning over my Underwood it was light outside.

"You look like shit, boy."

"Got run over by a crazed steer."

"Bob Fitzgerald called," Bart said, ignoring the fact that his halfman had been hit by a steer. The newsroom had that early before-the-storm quiet. Someone was eating a grilled cheese sandwich. I could smell it.

"So what's his problem now — typo in the obits?"

"No. The meeting with the state board on the bond issue was postponed. He's worried that all this unrest connected to the Jimmy Wilson story will affect the bond issue."

"Did you tell him it was just a little duck, casting a shadow?"

"Yeah, right. He wants to know why you're hyping the Jimmy Wilson story. I wouldn't discuss it with him anyway."

"So?"

"Well, the governor also called. Everyone's sick of the story. It isn't just Fitzgerald and advertisers anymore."

"Bart, you know damn well that I'm not making this shit up — I'm just covering the story. And I'm sick of the story. You know the governor's on the Zion board. Why doesn't he do the right thing and pressure the board to bury Jimmy?"

"You know that's not his style, to bulldoze hundreds of years of history. But I hear the Board of Supervisors is going to actually come to grips with the issue today. Be there."

"Can't stay away."

As I listened to Bart, the old feeling of grinding weariness turning into raw irritation stirred up again, and the all-day meeting of the board didn't help. Jimmy Wilson had forced them to realize that colored folk needed a new cemetery, they said, but getting to that realization was a difficult step. Turns out the inhabitants of Ashby were now immortal. Nobody could die because all the cemeteries were full up. Zion, they found out, was all sold out, too; even Potter's Field had maxed out in itinerant souls. I wondered if that had been the governor's strategy. The board had been talking the "special circumstance" to death for weeks. They revisited the history of Delaney Cemetery going back a hundred years to when Ashby County decided folks couldn't just bury their dead in the back yard and donated the land near the river for a colored cemetery. They located the old documents and found a precedent allowing a new land grant. Only one catch, it needed a signature from the Virginia governor. The story wrote itself.

Southern Comfort

Cissy Mae Fitzgerald was appointed to carry the document to Richmond in her capacity as City Planner, and she personally brought the huge maps over to The Sun so we could copy them. Her blond pageboy cut sort of whipped around her pretty face as she explained with emphasis which part of the land would be set aside for the new colored cemetery, her pearly pink fingernails tapping the map. We were sitting at the conference table in the newspaper's meeting room. It was after dark, and the old cast iron lamps in the corners barely lit the table. She spoke by turn in clichés about the cultural values

of the community and in an official voice about the importance of the Richmond trip.

"The governor you know…" Her hand brushed mine, and
I looked up from the map. Her gaze had lifted from the table,
and I held it for a moment before she stood up. "Why don't
you come too," she said. "That way you'll get the finale to the
story first-hand plus a photo of the governor signing the order."
Bart walked in as she hugged me goodbye, and I could tell he
didn't like the unusual familiarity.

"I'll drive," I said.

"No," she said. "I'll take care of that. Nite Bart."

Bart nodded goodnight.

It wasn't a hearse, but Cissy got one of those stretch Caddy
limos from the funeral parlor to ferry us to Richmond. I knew
the driver, Albert from the Club. Dear God, I thought, I don't
know his last name. Cissy pulled a drawstring and a grey
curtain wafted over the limo's partition.

We drove down the Valley on 81 and then a sharp turn east
on 64. The governor was flying to Tokyo that evening, so we
met in his study at the Executive Mansion. A lot of dark mahogany, but strangely out of place robin-egg blue walls gave some
relief. With pleasantries we were there half an hour and then
Cissy took us down to the Warf for dinner. We drank to the
success of the mission and drank some more. Virginia Gentleman Manhattans. "Here's to Jimmy Wilson, homeless no
more." Then she lit a Virginia Slims and pulled me out of the
restaurant.

It was late and I thought she would sleep all the way back
but she found a pint of Southern Comfort in the door next to
her, took a swig and passed it over. "Sorry, no ice," she said.
I let the syrupy burn trickle down my throat, and then Cissy's

lips sealed it all. The back seat was well recessed from the driver and she climbed on my lap, her tongue pushing Southern Comfort into my mouth, her hand grasping for my dick. She slid down and got it in her mouth and gripping it hard pushed me against the corner of the seat, and I wrestled with her, the pain from the football hit echoing sharply in my ribs, until I came and she lay back panting, pulling my hand between her legs, rubbing until I found the spot and then the muffled grunt. No business with the city planner ever came up after that day, and I never drank Southern Comfort again.

———

"So, what's the latest on Jimmy Wilson?" Clarke appeared, a wet print in her hand. "It's been weeks, and the poor man is still moping around in Quincy's back room."

I leaned forward, stretching my neck, feeling the ache shoot up from my waist. "The county board meeting was decisive, for a change." The springs twanged in the wood office chair as I reclined into the back pain. "Now that the governor signed, they finally decided to give Delaney Cemetery the land near the sewage treatment plant. Totally free, close to the old colored cemetery, but not right next to it. They're going to name it the Jimmy Wilson Annex."

"That's a hoot," she said. "A total nobody decides to get killed here, and we get a new colored cemetery. Well, at least that's the end of the story."

"They're wasting no time. He should be in the ground by nightfall. I want to get a shot of that before deadline."

It was already dark when I got there, but it wasn't hard to find Jimmy Wilson's resting place. The Annex was pasture-land, and the cattle, probably drawn by the unusual smell of fresh earth, had found and trampled the lone grave, spreading the dark soil back into the grass. A three-by-five-inch note card stuck on a popsicle stick was the only marker. It's too close to the river, I thought as I snapped the shots, careful to include the hoof prints, and then I nudged the Jeep out of the muddy field back onto the highway.

That's when I saw the whirling red, white and blue lights flashing toward me in the rear-view mirror. I hoped it was one of the cops I knew. I pulled over to the shoulder, stopping as the black sedan rolled up close behind me, lights blinding. I waited a moment and unlatched the seatbelt. Then a pickup truck came up fast, sliding into the gravel of the shoulder in front of my Jeep, blocking the way. Two men jumped out waving shotguns, their faces covered by hoods. They smashed my driver's side window with the gunstocks, yanked the door and pulled me out of the car like nothing. They were big men, Hessians. They didn't say anything as one of them pinned my arms from behind and the other one jammed the shotgun butt into my guts. As I jackknifed forward, heaving, the man slapped the shotgun barrel smartly across my forehead, just splitting the eyebrow above the bad eye, spraying some blood. Then they were back in the pickup, spitting gravel, speeding away. The police car was gone. I crawled back into the Jeep, crunching broken glass on the seat.

The emergency room was empty. No concussion. The eye was O.K. It was obvious they didn't want to cause heavy damage. They were surgical. It was only a few stitches, but I was there most of the night. I drove back to the newspaper and parked in the lot across from the pressroom. The early morning carriers were already loading up newspapers for the rural deliveries. Those papers would carry the finale, the end of the Jimmy Wilson story. He was in the ground now, in the muddy Annex, alone and away from all the other Ashby dead — the centuries old white and black dead and their frayed relationships.

The long hours and the beatings had worn me down like a sandblasting wind, sweeping away my very features. I hadn't been this tired, this close to the vanishing point, since Vietnam. Every move hurt, even the slightest grimace, but the pain felt almost reassuring. They couldn't waste me, and the eye is better, I thought. And then I realized that as much as they wanted the story to die, it hadn't died and now I couldn't let it die. Jimmy Wilson couldn't die.

I found the rope I needed, twenty feet of solid hemp weave almost an inch thick, and a spade in the newsprint storeroom and drove back toward the river, to the Jimmy Wilson Annex. I dug down and was surprised to hit the concrete cover of the vault just a foot into the soft earth. I cleared it off, swept the top clean and tied a square knot around an iron ring in the center of the slab. The Jeep spun in the mud, but I slammed it into four-wheel drive and the knobby tires dug in slowly pulling the slab out. I felt under a black tarp until I found a handle and I lifted one end of the coffin, propping it up out of the vault, tied the rope around the handle and pulled again with the Jeep until the box slid free on the mud. I backed the Jeep up close to the coffin and tipped it into the open back, sliding the box in. I pinned the tarp cover back in place and gunned the Jeep back out onto the highway. The sound of the road was deep and strong and suddenly it came to me — the Vietnam echo was gone. There was no more ringing in my head.

Away you rolling river

I cleaned my desk and left a goodbye note for Bart. I had a job in Miami, and I didn't want to face him. They were already talking about the weather story in the newsroom. The weather was the only hot news now that Jimmy Wilson's coffin had been found half hidden behind Ashby's gravestone over in Mount Zion Cemetery. Goldy hauled him back to the cemetery annex, and Jimmy had been resting peacefully for three weeks. A new aluminum marker with his name and dates graced the gravesite, now protected from the cattle by a chicken-wire fence.

It was morning, and the rain that had settled over Ashby all week was insistent, more abrasive now, and the gusts blew harder against the windshield as I strained to see the Route 7 blacktop. As I headed south, a tropical storm spinning reluctantly north out of the Gulf of Mexico churned up Appalachia, funneling along the Shenandoah Valley into Pennsylvania, toward Gettysburg. Clarke will cover it, I thought, knowing I would miss her.

Heading east to I-95, I passed Goldy's black-and-white parked at the bridge, all lights flashing, and crossing the Shenandoah, I saw the water already cresting high above its banks, covering the low-lying slopes, flooding the sewage treatment plant and the Jimmy Wilson Annex of the Delaney Cemetery. Climbing the horseshoe bend into the Blue Ridge, I finally lost sight of the river.

Behind me, the water rushed white, reaching high, higher than ever before, high above the old watermarks on the leaning oak trees, dragging broken branches and shattered trailers. As I heard later, the relentless current sucked Jimmy's coffin out from the vault in the fresh earth and carried it downriver, ripping the black tarp cover from the brass nails, until a frantic twisting branch reaching low snared it. Later, when the storm weakened and the water receded, the coffin remained perched high on the tree, the shredded cover flapping like the wings of a great dark bird.

CHAPTER TWO

The Summer of Sight and Sound

The war, the war...the war, the war.
— ABUELO

El Tio Chevo

It was almost summer and Christmas, always bright-hot as the rainy season ends in Costa Rica, beckoned me again as I walked through my childhood neighborhood in San José, eliciting memories that awakened old misgivings, reminding me that I never wanted to return. But now I was on assignment.

Abuelo would give me one colón every day of Christmas, and I'd race my new Raleigh 26-incher with gears and dynamo past Plaza Víquez for miles into downtown and to a corner hole-in-the-wall news shop near the Parque Central to buy a superhero comic book every day and sit in the Parque Central looking at the images because I couldn't read the words and the other chiquillos would run up and squealing grab my Christmas comics and run away only to bring them back because they were in English.

Now, Christmas-time again thirty years later, I stood in front of a lean-to, near the Bellavista Fortress that loomed dirty-yellow and pockmarked with bullet holes over San José and my childhood. Uncle Chevo's home was an alley between two houses, covered by sheets of tin roofing, a window and a front door with iron rejas cut into two plywood four-by-eights. A young woman opened the barred door. She was a pretty girl, twenty, no more, slightly plump, short dark hair and porcelain-doll white skin, barefooted in a plain dress. She beckoned, and I stepped up a high step to a raised wooden platform into a room divided by a thin calico curtain, its faded bluish print ballooning with the breeze, revealing the corner of a plastic-covered mattress resting on the floor in front of a seatless commode. A two-burner stovetop, a rubber sink and a small paint-splotched desk with two small chairs crowded the front of the room. A single bulb shining weakly swayed on a long cord hanging from the crossbeam that supported the tin roof.

"Ya viene," she said.

A large sledgehammer head on the desk, perhaps a twenty-pounder, held down a few yellow legal-pad sheets with penciled scratches that looked like formulas and a diagram with carefully marked spaces inside a rectangle. I remembered Chevo as a perennial adolescent, spoiled by his father's wealth, and by the look of it now barely surviving on the margin of a world that he had inherited whole. I last saw him at Julia's funeral. He was dressed in a pressed black gabardine suit and a starched white shirt with the collar buttoned so tightly the tips curled up. My mother had fallen, suffered a cerebral hemorrhage and spent her last two months in and out of consciousness at the Calderón public hospital. Hans, Fritz and tía Rosita cared for her in the neurosurgery ward, but Chevo never went.

After her funeral, I sat with him, nursing *ron colorado* in La Lora. He just didn't want to see her like that, Chevo had said, and I suppressed the urge to get up and walk away from the old man, but stayed out of fatigue more than anything, and Chevo sipped rum and told a story of Julia's childhood, how she cracked her head on a swing and how he saved her, how she once scalded herself with boiling beans. Then he coughed and spat a perfect silver dollar of phlegm at the tile floor as if he were aiming to miss the caulk lines. A little woman appeared instantly with a bucket and mop — she looked like the mop in its colorless motion — wiped it up and disappeared. Not saying anything, I put a twenty-dollar bill on the table and walked away.

At the door, I saw Chevo pluck the bill and stuff it into his shirt pocket. After that, I just wanted to forget him, Costa Rica and mom's squalid death in the public hospital. All that was ten years ago and so much has happened. I could have been killed in Nam or lynched by good old boys in Virginia, so far, so distant from this little country in Central America, and they never would have known. I never came back until the newspaper sent me now, and a gentle tug that came out of nowhere had pulled me over to my uncle's lean-to.

First I heard the family whistle outside. It was the song of the quetzal. Chucha went to the door. "Tu sobrino," your nephew, she said. Then Chevo burst in with a loud cheerful "Hola, muchacho," as he clapped two dripping beer bottles and a soda on the desk and gave me a powerful hug. "Todo un atleta, miralo." Built like an athlete, he said. He smiled with his whole face. His hair was still dark, and at more than sixty-five he was still robust and muscular. He looked the way I remembered, the way he always looked, even back then,

29

that summer when I went with Abuelo to get him out of San Lucas penitentiary.

"¿Cuántos han sido, veinte años, verdad?" How many years, twenty? Chevo said.

"Diez, solamente, desde mamá." Only ten, since mom.

"Oh, sí." He paused. "What brings you back now?" He smiled, mixing English into the conversation, proud of his English.

"Ahora soy periodista," I said. "I'm writing about politics."

"Politics. Me cago en todo. Bullshit. How long are you here?"

"Couple of days. Interviewing the Archbishop of Managua pasado mañana, then to Guatemala."

"What's happening in Guatemala?"

"Massacre in a little village called Salta Tigre."

"The Army? It's always those cabrones."

"Sí, parece que sí, la misma mierda de siempre, the same old bullshit. Then back to Miami. ¿Y la muchacha? Who is she?"

"Chucha. I found her one day, en el bus que va pa Turrialba. Es nica from Nicaragua, and she's alone. She liked me y se quedó." They finished the beers. Chevo said he was now living the ultimate irony, an agronomist without land.

"And the farm in Las Pavas?"

"Rosita won't let me back until I marry Chucha. But we can't. There's still Mariana in Cartago."

"Claro, Mariana...and your daughter?"

Yes, he was now a grandfather too, but with no money to buy any land and no job because he always lost his temper at injustice, he said. One of the other agronomists at the center for tropical agriculture questioned the accuracy of his theories about corn hybrids, he said, and after the meeting Chevo shoved the startled man against a car and challenged him to a duel.

"Con el smithanweson, carajo. Tengo una puntería brutal con el smithanwesson," I'm a hell of a shot with the Smith and Wesson, he said. "Se cagó en los pantalones, shit in his pants and they fired me."

He opened the top drawer of the desk, took out an old blue-black Smith and Wesson .38-caliber revolver and aimed it at the ceiling. "Donde pongo el ojo, pongo la bala," Where I see it, I hit it, he said.

His fingers, the nails blackened, rubbed the gun's oily finish as he talked. He didn't own anything now, he said, just the gun, his inventions and the hammerhead he lifted to strengthen his arms. We went behind the shack to a small patch of ground that matched the rectangle on the legal pad. Six corn stalks were his inventions. La Nación had even reported it, he said. They produced twice as much corn as the usual Costa Rican plants.

"I remember your fields in Las Pavas," I said, "and the summer Abuelo took me along to bring you home from San Lucas."

"Claro que sí. Me acuerdo perfectamente, a vivid memory."

We would spend summers at the family farm near Turrialba — about a hundred kilometers east of San José, beyond the mountain range that rings the capital, on the other side of the Irazú volcano heading toward the Atlantic coast, toward the port of Limón on the Reventazón River, amid endless dwarf coffee trees growing right up to the rain forest — and joined the harvest picking the ripe red berries with the gangs of boys in white shirts and blue pants and girls in full white cotton skirts and red bandanas, laughing and flirting, singing school songs. "Don't eat those berries," Chevo would say. "They'll give you the cagazón." There was also sugar cane and some land set aside for Chevo's experiments, just enough, maybe two hectares for his hybrid corn and special coffee.

Chevo always bickered with the neighbor to the south over the shifting fence line and over the neighbor's half-wild dogs. It was an old feud dating back decades to the day Abuelo accepted the farm in payment for a legal debt. Maricón de mierda, fucking asshole, Chevo yelled out one day, offending the neighbor in a way that could not be overlooked. Then the cabrón and another fool ambushed him on the road to Turrialba, Chevo remembered with a smile, rubbing his left palm. One of them held a rifle on him and the other raised his machete, hesitating a moment, and Chevo grabbed it by the blade severing the tendons in his left hand and in almost the same motion hitting the man's face with the blade, slashing into his right cheek, laying bare all the man's teeth.

A machete is a heavy tool, a clumsy weapon in a close fight, Chevo said. It needs weight and speed behind it to be effective. He did the best he could, he said. The second man fired, missed, and Chevo whacked off his left forearm and grabbed the rifle. El colmo, Chevo said, was that he had to get his horse and take both men to town for treatment. Then he turned himself in and was locked up for about a year until Abuelo and I came looking for him that summer.

Mi pobre culito

I liked the memory and my anger at the old man started to fade.

"¿Te acuerdas de los perros?" Remember the dogs? Chevo said.

I was only six or so that summer and small. When the bus from Turrialba dropped them off near the farm, the neighbor's lanky, malnourished mongrels, about five or six, rushed toward us barking and we had no weapons. Abuelo and Chevo pulled off their belts, and I tried to squeeze between them. They lashed at the snarling dogs with the belts, and Chevo felled one with a good kick.

"One of the saguates got you on the culo," Chevo said.

"Sí, me acuerdo. And later you poured rum on my butt to clean the bite."

"Tu pobre culito," Chevo said. "Your little butt took one helluva bruising that summer. That's why you were with papá that day and most of the summer. Remember that pervert, don't you?"

"I don't remember much, just spending the whole summer with Abuelo."

"Interesting how memory works, isn't it?"

"What do you mean?"

"You remember me in prison, one year of my life out of sixty-five, and I remember your pobre culito, one moment out of your life."

"I know. It's not fair, is it?"

I had been out of school for about a month. Chevo recalled the timing because that was right before we showed up to spring him from jail. He would never forget Abuelo's anger. The old man was so proud of me, the first nieto, born on the day Hitler killed himself. Abuelo found Julia crying and she showed him the torn underpants smeared in blood.

"And they took me to Dr. Saborío to stitch up my little asshole and mom screamed more than I did."

"You would never say anything about the rape to anybody."

They never found the guy who did it. They asked and begged, but I never would say. He would have castrated that jueputa, Chevo said, before he put a bullet in the jueputa's head.

"We called you Sereno, remember, because you were such a quiet kid living in your own microscopic world. In the American school, they thought you were retarded, but then that was also the summer we discovered you were practically blind and deaf."

"Yes, when Abuelo took me to the doctor, and the doctor noticed I couldn't see shit or hear well, and I remember the day I got the glasses at the Óptica Mora."

That time was a blur, but as Chevo talked, I started to see flashes of images and realized that I had never really forgotten the rape, but that it had remained obscured, secluded in a blurred, echoing place in the long darkness before that summer, the summer Abuelo gave me sight and sound. It was tucked away with all the reasons why I never wanted to come back. Julia and Abuelo were dead, anyway. Their deaths were tucked away too.

I walked away from Chevo's little house and looked up at the massive fort on the hill that overlooked the barrios to orient myself, just as I had as a child. The yellow fortress, shot full of holes during the revolution of 1948 was always there and so were the immense black cypresses in front of the Iglesia de la Soledad where I took my first communion and had to tell the priest that I loved to kiss the maid Zulema's breasts and play in the wet softness between her legs.

I walked in the early evening down the narrow quiet streets. Grandfather's old house was still there, washed-out green, on a corner, now divided into apartments. I noticed the old scars where a Jeep had crashed through the corner wall into the living room, shattering abuela's Dresden. Around the corner and a few houses down, I found Carlitos' rowhouse. Carlitos was a great soccer player at St. Francis and the kids respected him and hung around his house and kicked a soccer ball in the street. Walking up to the house, right up close to the door, I could see the wood grain, and I knocked and waited, but there was no answer.

Fishermen still sold lobsters by the hundreds on the side-walks of the Avenida Central, green-black monsters waving their claws at me as I pushed through crowds of Christmas shoppers over to the cantina La Lora on the Parque Central where Abuelo used to drink *ron colorado* with his cronies. La Lora opened up like an enormous airplane hangar to the dark green murmuring royal palms of the twilight park now drip-ping in tiny white lights, teenage girls walking around arm in arm throwing confetti and dozens of shoeshine boys engaged in fantastic deals over worn comic books, chasing customers and giving each other sidekicks. Waiters in white jackets hurried around, bending toward the seated clients, rushing back and forth to the bar, the round trays tilting high above their heads always threatening to spill, but they never did.

When the old man and his pals drank straight *ron colorado* with water chasers in La Lora that summer, I would sit there too with new eyeglasses, horn-rimmed just like Abuelo's, listening to stories of political treachery I really couldn't under-stand, but understanding that some were cabrones and others jueputas and he'd laugh with the viejos and eat the little pieces of blue-white palmito asado with mayonnaise and lemon the waiter would bring with the rum.

Abuelo kept me close that summer, the summer I really got to know my grandfather, as the old man told the old stories, usually reliving them with anger, sometimes with loving sadness. La guerra, la guerra, he would say, and I would say what war, what war, and he would say la guerra, la guerra, telling how the militia led by his own brother-in-law and the traitor Rojas had chased him to Turrialba, shooting at him as he fled into the cafetales and Rojas putting the gun to his head, and how Macedonio, the Indian wood-carver, kept him hidden in a cave for weeks, feeding him and nursing his wound, swimming the Reventazón River to bring food until there was no danger. And then, the war, the war that brought my father and the Germans to the farm, the war.

I just hung on to Abuelo's hand and went along everywhere, and we brought Chevo home from San Lucas Penitentiary, a massive white and blue fort with gigantic wood slabs for doors painted indigo and red, guarded by uniformed men with drawn sabers. Chevo was waiting right inside the doors, sitting with other inmates on the straw-littered floor. Through my horn-rimmed abuelito glasses I examined the lush detail, the dirty-yellow straw, the blue-white walls, the steel flash of the sabers.

I could see. I remembered the instant. Abuelo took me to la Óptica Mora, and they fitted the tortoise-shell rims with thick lenses just like Abuelo's around his ears. One ear is higher than the other, Mora said as he worked, and when Mora moved aside I could see the glass door and the dirt on the glass door and the cars rushing by outside on the Avenida Central, and I didn't talk much for days. Chevo and Julia laughed and called me abuelito. No more Sereno. After the doctor pulled the stitches from my culito, he looked into my ears. Es una selva, a jungle in there, he said. The nurse held my tousled head in a vise-grip and the doctor shot a rush of warm water into each ear with a massive stainless-steel syringe and long black plugs popped out, letting the crashing sounds of the city roll in. I ran to the window searching wildly for the source of the roaring waves.

At the end of the summer, I rode my Christmas bike over to the Parque Central and saw the boys gathered for the first time before they saw me and before they could push me down and run away with the comic books, and sitting on the grass — I could see the very spot now from La Lora — I looked at the color images in a new Superman comic book and suddenly realized I could read the English words.

"¿Limpia, señor?" A barefooted boy in worn cut-off pants and a huge T-shirt came around and plopped a shoeshine kit next to my shoes, handing me a newspaper.

"Tico Times, ¿cuánto?" I said.

"English, English. Léalo, se lo presto."

I pointed to my Timberland boat shoes. "¿Sábes como limpiar éstos?"

"Claro, todos lo gringos los usan, gringo shoes. Son búfalo. Yo sé como limpiar búfalo."

I smiled at him, all the gringos wear buffalo hide shoes, and he knows how to polish them. I nodded at him to go ahead. I spotted a photo on the front page of the English language newspaper of a man, his arm in a sling, next to two other men holding M-16 rifles and under it a one-line headline over the caption:

Ramírez Survives Assassination Attempt

GUATEMALA CITY – The socialist former mayor of Guatemala City, Carlos Ramírez, one of three candidates campaigning in the presidential primaries leading up to the 1980 election, narrowly escaped assassination here yesterday in front of his house in a fashionable section of the city. He was slightly injured by shots fired from a passing car. His wife and two daughters were inside the house and were not hurt.

"Dos pesos," the shoeshine boy said. I gave him an extra colón for the paper.

Ramírez had been Chevo's student at Turrialba's Inter-American Institute for Agricultural Sciences, agriculture minister in Guatemala and later mayor of the Guatemala City. Because of that connection, he had been my source for more than a year. It's a violent country, but as a presidential candidate, Ramírez had received more death threats than usual, and he worried about it. I crossed through the crowded Parque Central to the Western Union office and wired Rosenfeld, the managing editor at the paper in Miami.

> Rosy, Skipping Managua. Going straight to
> Guatemala City. In Hotel Panamericano
> Thursday. Helpful if you wire me U.S.
> State Department lowdown on Ramírez
> shooting. Working on follow-up and maybe
> presidential interview on Salta Tigre.
> Home Friday. Regards, Harding.

La Chucha was gone. Chevo sensed that we were now on better terms, and he promised to show up in Miami someday. He gave me a strong goodbye hug, and I returned the abrazo.

"Saludame a Ramírez."

"Claro."

I walked away, turning and waving at the lone man barefooted in front of an alley with a tin roof. It was like finally walking away without rancor from Costa Rica itself.

CHAPTER THREE

Land of Eternal Spring

Le dolía su país como si le hubiera podrido la sangre.
Le dolía afuera y en la médula, en la raíz del pelo,
bajo las uñas, entre los dientes.
— MIGUEL ÁNGEL ASTURIAS, *EL SEÑOR PRESIDENTE*

The Socialist

Uncomfortable in a white linen suit, Jonas Harding hurried through Juan Santamaría Airport just making the earliest Lacsa flight to Guatemala City. Lacsa scheduled flights on a 24-hour clock, and he'd misread the ticket. He had scheduled a mid-afternoon interview with Ramírez — too tight, but Ramírez insisted on that timing.

The Boeing 737 was packed. He spotted his empty middle seat and jammed in between two women, sticking an elbow into the ribs of the one in the window seat. She started out of a doze.

"Sorry."

"No matter," she said.

He slipped the Olivetti under the seat, in front of his feet.

"Typewriter?" she said.

"Yea, I write for a living. Reporter." He wrestled with his jacket. She leaned back and helped pull one arm out. Pretty woman, he thought, in a harsh sort of way. "Thanks, glad to get rid of that." She smiled, watched the city disappear below and lit a Marlboro the moment the no-smoking sign went off. Her light brown hair was cut short into a severe crow's wing that covered part of her face — small features, thin lips and smooth skin with an indoor pallor — as she leaned toward him and handed him a card — Sally Beardsly, a travel agent from San Francisco on a group junket sponsored by the Office for Central American Tourism to revisit the land of eternal spring and sell it to her clients.

"Guatemala's safe again," she said, "and, oh, so beautiful. Have you seen Tikal?"

"Never been there."

She dozed again and her head slipped onto his shoulder. Scent of oranges and tobacco in her hair. Her folded hands were translucent white with tapered fingers, unpolished, carefully manicured nails. A Victorian ring with three small emeralds inlaid in gold held an almost invisible wedding band in place.

The flight to Guatemala lasted about an hour. As the plane touched down she said she was staying at the Intercontinental and why not have dinner? The other agents were a bore, she said. He followed her slim figure as she hurried off the plane. Then she turned and waved, "Eight o'clock." She stopped for a moment to evaluate the figure of the man — average height, dark brown hair, skin a shade darker than hers, perhaps from the tropical sun, broad shoulders and an athletic gait. "O.K.," she said to herself.

Harding checked into the Panamericano, a quiet old hotel in the heart of Guatemala City, where the staff still wore the flowing colors of Mayan costume. Rosenfeld's telex reply waited in the room with a fruit basket from the manager.

> Jonas, Ramírez's attack and wound
> unconfirmed by U.S. State calls shooting a
> hoax, typical of Guatemalan presidential
> politics. Don't come back till Monday. Relax
> a little. Rosy.

"¿No va a almorzar, señor Jonas?" the manager called after him.

"No tengo tiempo, gracias."

It was a cool, bright afternoon as the taxi drove through a compression of shops and a blue and dirty-yellow marketplace jammed with Mayan faces, then through suburban streets and up the hills to a classy neighborhood of walled villas. The driver pointed to a house, about a block away, but refused to drive any closer. Jonas didn't insist. Walking up to a wide circular driveway and the carefully tended garden of the villa, he noticed the shadows of two men rushing into the house, then Ramírez stepping out of the front door, the film-star smile broad, his left arm in a sling. He put his right hand on Jonas's shoulder.

"Adelante, Jonas. Los demás andan de compras." The others are out shopping.

"And them?"

"Bodyguards. Don't worry. You won't even see them."

"It's getting more dangerous here all the time. They won't rest until they kill you."

41

"Let's talk out here. The house is bugged."

"And you live with that? Get somebody to clean it out."

"The ones who clean it out do the bugging. I had it swept out and two days later it was all back in place. They don't even believe I was shot." He lifted his bandaged arm.

"I know. The U.S. believes you made it up."

"The only thing I can do is leave Guatemala for a while."

"How's that?"

"I'm dropping out of the race."

"Can I print that?"

"I'd like to announce it here first."

"Sure, just give me a heads up. And now what will you do?"

"I'm taking Angelina and the girls to Paris for a while."

"What's in Paris?"

"I have a job offer, UNESCO."

"Doing what?"

"Hanging out with the other exiled ex-ministers and political refugees with good connections." He laughed and then coughed. "I owe it to my family. Since the beginning of the campaign, we've been tutoring the girls at home. They're tired of that."

"What about Salta Tigre. You made it an issue. It won't go away, especially in Washington, just because you quit the campaign."

"At this point I don't want to go on the record, for obvious reasons. What's the point, agreed?"

"Yes, de acuerdo."

"At first I only said that the story didn't make sense. The Interior Ministry said guerrillas had massacred the people and razed the village. But there's been no guerrilla activity anywhere near Salta Tigre. Later, one survivor, maybe the only one, came to me. He'd seen Army regulars kill those people and burn down their village. And he saw them shoot the American priest."

"Can I talk to him?"

"No. He'd be dead the moment you walk out the door, but I have very detailed notes. When are you leaving?"

"I have an interview with the president day after tomorrow. I leave that afternoon."

"Come by tomorrow morning. I'll have copies of the papers for you, for publication after I'm in Europe."

"Está bien."

"I'll call a cab. Pick it up a block down the hill."

"Yes. I know. By the way, Chevo sends regards."

"I love that viejo verde."

———

Harding called the Intercontinental and she said come on over, that she was drawing a bath. She answered the knock wrapped in a towel.

"There's rum and ice on the night table. Get a drink and keep me company."

Jonas poured a shot of La Negrita and followed her into the steaming bathroom.

"Have a seat," she said. She brought his hand with the glass up to her mouth, took a long sip of the iced straight rum looking at his eyes and turned, letting the towel fall to the tile. Her thigh brushed his lips as she stepped into the bathwater.

The Cuban

Ramírez's tone of relief still lingered in Harding's mind the next day as he paid the taxi and walked up to the walled villa. The morning was bright but cold. The circular driveway was packed with military vehicles and soldiers with M-16s. Inside the garden, a wall of soldiers surrounded him, shoving him toward a handsome, fleshy man with swept-back black hair. The man looked relaxed, bemused, an Uzi hanging loosely from the left shoulder of his white, long-sleeved guayabera. Jonas thought he recognized the face but couldn't place it.

"What's your problem, asshole?" Guayabera said.

"No problem, sir. I have an appointment with Carlos Ramírez."

"If you want to talk to him, it is a problem and maybe only the first problem."

"What's going on here?"

"Let's start with the problem. You are the fucking problem," Guayabera said moving closer, his face red, angry. Stepping back, only to bump into an unyielding police officer, Jonas struggled to find a card in the jacket. A clanking of hardware made him freeze. He looked up slowly at the row of M-16s. "Just a card, amigos. Sólo una tarjeta," he said, tugging the card gently out of the jacket and handing it to Guayabera.

"Look. I'm a reporter from Miami, and I have an appointment."

Guayabera stared at the card for a long moment, fingering the Uzi with his left hand. "Oh. You're Harding, meeting with the president tomorrow morning."

"That's right. How'd you know that?"

"We've been expecting you. I'm Manolo Rosales, chief of presidential security, and I clear all the boss's visitors."

"What's Ramírez got to do with presidential security?"

"Vamos, chico, I'll show you what this war's all about."

"You're Cuban."

"Hey, and you're from Miami, chico. We're exiliados in a fucked-up land."

Jonas followed Rosales into the luxurious home, through an expansive foyer into the dining room where Ramírez, his wife and two thin adolescent girls sat at the table, slouching forward, their faces on the tablecloth in pooling blood.

"Don't touch that." Rosales said, as Jonas groped the table for support. "My God," Jonas said. "He told me he'd dropped out, that he was headed to Paris to UNESCO."

"Communists never drop out."

"He was a Social Democrat."

"What's the fucking difference, chico?"

Jonas looked up, squinting, half-blinded. His knees and hands could not stop shaking.

"Come on. I'll drive you back to the Panamericano," Rosales said.

Even in his weakened state, Jonas remembered that he had not mentioned the Panamericano.

On the way, Rosales pulled over to a café near the main marketplace. "Vamos a tomar algo," he said.

They sat in a corner from where Jonas could see the street and the hubbub of the market. Rosales unbuttoned his guayabera, took the car keys and a paperback book from a side-pocket and placed them on the edge of the table. Jonas could see part of the title under the keys. *Early Poems*, e.e. cummings. The waiter brought two coffees and they sipped quietly.

"How'd you end up here?" Jonas said. He was struggling to stop shaking, to think of something to say to this man.

"I wouldn't say that I've ended up anywhere yet." He spoke softly, as if forgetting the scene in Ramirez's dining room. "The CIA trained me for the Bay of Pigs. After the invasion, after I got out of the Cuban prison, I worked for the Venezuelans. Had to leave the U.S. to find work."

"You were there when the Cubana plane blew up two years ago?"

"I was. Then my contacts in U.S. intelligence hooked me up here."

"Family in Cuba?"

"My stepmother."

"And Miami?"

"Yes, family — brother, ex-wife and kid. She runs Laura's Café on Eighth Street. You've probably been there. Your newspaper is opening an office right across from the café."

"Yes, I know her. I go there often. Didn't know she was your ex and didn't know about the newspaper office."

Rosales's eyes crinkled a little as he looked at Jonas. "Sorry, thinking of my wife."

A paperboy came up to the table.

"¿Prensa Libre?"

"No," Rosales said.

"Dos por uno," two for the price of one, the boy said looking at Jonas.

"No joda, váyase," Rosales said.

"Regáleme algo," give me a little something, the boy said.

"Ven acá," Rosales said. The boy came over and handed Rosales the paper. Rosales rolled it up and swatted the boy smartly on the nose. The boy stumbled back, more surprised than hurt. "Jueputa," sonofabitch, the boy said.

"Ahora sí, vete," now go, Rosales said.

"Jueputa," the boy said not moving. Rosales stood and the boy grabbed the paper and scampered. Jonas sipped the last of the coffee, studying Rosales.

"You knew I was staying at the Panamericano."

"We check up on all the boss's visitors. It's a dangerous town. Couple of weeks ago, an old guy named Prieto, owner of a brewery, was having lunch right here, at this table, with his wife and two bodyguards. Over there, near the window, three university students were drinking beer and bullshitting around, cussing a little. The old man didn't like the cussing. 'Oigan, respeten a mi señora,' he said and one of the kids yelled back, 'no joda, viejo de mierda,' and the old man pulled out his gun and shot him. The bodyguards, startled by the shot, opened fire killing all three kids. Normally, here that would've been the end of it, but the boys weren't chusma. They were upper-crust kids, and the incident came all the way up to the president. By the time I got involved, Prieto was already shot dead, anyway."

"Drop me off at the Panamericano," Jonas said. "I've got a story to write."

The secretary and the colonel

As a child, Gabriela Jones lived right over the water on the sewage-covered inlet-edges of Belize's Caribbean coast in a small plywood cabin built on stilts. She remembered digging her toes in the muddy sand of the narrow beach in the evenings, thinking of escape as the setting sun or a bright moon rippled along under the house. When her mother threw out the garbage, the water erupted into lighted starbursts as tiny, silvered fish jumped in a frenzy, fighting for scraps through the shimmering film of shit. They lived on sewage like the fish, somehow surviving. Sometimes a fish would jump high and land on the flimsy porch, and she would find it there dead in the morning. First, she would examine it like a hungry cat, then she would usually kick it away, thinking, *You are finally free.* Her prison walls were on both sides — on one side the sea, on the other the jungles that grew beyond even her imagination at first — but then at fifteen she realized that the holding walls were also the doorways to freedom, and she followed the single highway for weeks, walking through the lacerating scrub brush on foot, crossing from Belize into Guatemala, until a military patrol picked her up, dehydrated and exhausted. The soldiers raped her and left her near Guatemala City. There, scrounging through garbage, she was found by Doña Teodora, the wife of the man who would become president. That was thirty years ago, and Gabriela was still with them, a black woman in a Mayan country, secretary to a mestizo president.

Protected now, insulated by distance and time, she liked to think about those days. Thinking back made the present that much sweeter, steeling her to do her duty, which she did without question, without rancor and with some pleasure. An attractive middle-aged woman with small chiseled features and thoughtful hazel-brown eyes that seldom smiled, she knew the president's secrets, protected him from his enemies and quietly procured the adolescent nephews he favored. She found the president's nephews, bathed them, clothed them and afterward returned them home estrenando ropa, with new clothes and toys and with money for the family. The thoughts of the barefoot girl faded away as she flipped through the pages of her Moroccan leather agenda and highlighted three names for the day's appointments: The American journalist, Jonas Harding, Manolo Rosales and Army chief of staff Colonel Nathaniel Watson.

––––––––

Watson walked in brisk steps through the echoing shaded halls of the presidential palace, shoulder to shoulder with Rosales.

"Bad timing on the Ramírez deal," Watson said.

"I know, but this is Guatemala, chief."

"It's more than just a little inconvenient to have an American reporter for a major publication walk in on the Ramírez scene. I'm giving him a guided tour at Salta Tigre tomorrow, and now he's got two massacres to write about. That could have an effect in Washington."

"Look, a situation like this is like delivering a baby. Timing is subject to contractions."

"You're the doctor, Manolo, but from what I heard, it was more like an abortion."

"Look chief, it looked like grace before dinner. But you are right. It should have been only Ramírez. The fucking Indian went nuts."

When Rosales saw them dead at the table, Vargas standing behind them, his face revealing nothing, he lunged forward and yanked the smaller man toward him, pummeling his face bloody until Vargas collapsed, uttering only one word, "Gabriela." When Jonas showed up, Rosales took him to the killings out of anger, in retribution. It wasn't much, but something, even that… The fucking demon whore, he thought, she told him to waste them all.

Watson stopped, catching his breath. "We've been pretty lucky. The Associated Press already ran the story, and there wasn't much reaction and the consulate read me Harding's story in today's Miami paper. It was to the point, no more, and maybe he won't write anything else anyway." Rosales grasped Watson's arm, perhaps too firmly. "You want to explain that." It wasn't a question.

"What if he doesn't come back from Salta Tigre? The cover story still holds. Marxist guerrillas wiped out Salta Tigre, right?" Watson said.

"Go on."

"And Salta Tigre is still hot, right?"

"No. Even the U.S. Embassy says there's no guerrilla activity there, and Harding knows that," Rosales said.

"Of course they know that, and we know that, but guerrillas are unpredictable and, well, what if it really heats up again? I guess everybody'll be surprised. That's what we need to draw more American money to fight the guerrillas. It won't be the first time an American reporter in Central America was blown away by guerrillas. I just have to make sure Harding finds the commie bastards."

"What did the President say?"

"It was Gabriela's idea," Watson said.

"Shit."

Watson picked up the pace, leaving Rosales behind as he entered the cavernous kitchen where Gabriela waited for their meeting, over coffee. He shared an English language intimacy with her, understood only to them, cemented when she helped him overcome the initial resentment in the Army over the appointment of a Honduran to head the joint chiefs. He had no confidence in Rosales. He distrusted religious fanatics and to him Cuban exiles were religious fanatics. Although he had been out of pocket, near the Mexican border all week, he had approved her plan to deal with Ramírez. But it worried him. I won't be the president's buggered boy on this, he thought as he and Rosales joined her at the massive wooden kitchen table.

Rosales noted that without the president's usual presence, there were no native Guatemalans at the meeting. The boss doesn't trust his own blood, he thought.

"I understand Harding walked right in on the Ramírez's crime scene," Gabriela said.

"I know it was unfortunate," Rosales said.

Watson looked at Gabriela.

"It couldn't have been worse timing if it had been planned that way," she said.

"It had to be a target of opportunity," Rosales said. He knew Watson liked the jargon. "They did go too far —."

"Skip it," she said. "What did they discuss the day before?"

"Salta Tigre, of course," Rosales said.

"Any mention of a Cuban?"

Watson glanced at Gabriela. He hadn't heard about a Cuban. She glanced back. Just go with it, the glance said.

"It was hard to hear," Rosales said. "They were outside, but no, I don't think Ramírez said anything about a Cuban."

"You really think Ramírez was that plugged in with Havana?" Watson said.

"I'm convinced of it," she said, "The wiretaps showed some Havana insight."

"I never trust the gringo wiretap reports," Watson said. "He always knew the house was bugged."

"Well, we want Harding to know about the Cuban now," she said. "A Cuban's really good for us at this point. He gives us a new focus, shifting the issue for the gringos from humanitarian outrage into a new threat."

"Where'd they spot the Cuban?" Rosales said.

"The Americans reported him crossing over from Honduras, a week ago, she said. We can give Harding that story now. It's fresh. He can confirm the sighting with the gringos, and he'll leave the Ramírez thing alone for now. Let him draw his own conclusions about that."

"Anyway, ultimately, it'll all need fixing – Ramírez, Salta Tigre, all of it," Watson said.

"How do we fix it?" Rosales said.

"Harding runs into the Cuban at Salta Tigre and that fixes it," she said.

"The Cuban who's nowhere near Salta Tigre," Rosales said.

"Claro," she said, "that's our job. To get that Cuban to Salta Tigre and have him take care of Harding."

"The timing's all wrong," Rosales said.

"Sure," Watson said, "but by the time Harding figures that out, it's all over, one way or another."

"It's all about gaining the advantage and cooling things down for us right now," she said. She looked down at her hands.

Watson stared at her. He knew she liked the idea of turning bad PR into a victory of sorts. When he saw her like that he thought of a ballerina's feet. He thought of a beautiful female animal dancing effortlessly on hard-calloused feet, leaping and pivoting airborne as if suspended from water-hardened leather and hemp taut as a hangman's noose. She lifted her face and touched his hand under the table. He understood the tremu-lous touch of her hand.

"What's wrong?" she glanced at Rosales.

"We're fighting a civil war with fronts on all sides. Thousands have died. Why waste time with this bullshit?" Rosales said.

"Yes, it's a detail," she said. "But it's a thorn. I need to pull that thorn. You know that."

"Ultimately nobody gives a shit about Salta Tigre," Rosales said, "or Ramírez, for that matter."

"We can use that and I want to be sure," she said.

Rosales walked away thinking that their preferred way to transform the mess they were in into a win by trapping the reporter at Salta Tigre was bound to fail. He was tired of their twisted logic. Harding's presence made him think of Miami. He thought of Laura in black and white and red — white skin, black hair, black eyes, the fire engine red fingernails and the somehow rosy pastel of her lips always as if to kiss, the sideways glance and the full throaty laugh that shook her and him as she pulled his arms and then pressed herself against him like an avalanche.

El Señor Presidente

The president liked to receive American journalists in his private den in the basement of the presidential palace. A small personal office filled with ham-radio equipment, sometimes a nephew present, provided an informal, almost intimate setting, and he could tell from the articles afterward that the gringos responded well to the ambiance. He knew that Gabriela was nervous about the informality of these interviews, but he liked the challenge of sizing up the man, understanding his point of view, and then using it to advantage. The private study gave him that edge. The foreign reporters didn't expect it. They anticipated seeing a formal setting and a military uniform.

He glanced again at Rosales's account of Harding's activities:

*The reporter registered at the Hotel Panamericano
and then met Ramírez. Harding then had dinner at the
Hotel Intercontinental with Sally Beardsly, a travel
agent from San Francisco and spent the night there.
The next morning he walked in on the Ramírez crime
scene, went back to the Panamericano and an hour
later to Western Union to telex a story on the killings,
(attached).*

Salta Tigre had been the main item on Harding's agenda, the president thought, claro, before Ramírez, and now both were connected, but perhaps there was an opportunity to turn that around. Watson would clean up the mess. He had done it before.

The guard led Jonas Harding through a large hall, painted royal blue and gold, brilliant in the morning sunlight, down a thin dark stairwell into the basement. The president, short and stout in late middle age, wearing a maroon bathrobe and a huge earphone headset, sat in front of a wall of ham-radio equipment, fiddling with dials. A thin young man, no more than a teenager, stood behind him, his hands on the president's shoulders. The president turned to Jonas, waving at the radio equipment.

"My toy...connects me to the world. Welcome, Mr. Harding. Está en su casa."

He gave Harding an enthusiastic handshake, slapping him on the shoulder. The president pulled off the earphones, brushing his hair back into place. It was too black for his age and strangely long, growing from the left temple, sweeping to the right, over the bald spot.

"Anda, Julito, búscanos un cafecito," get us a coffee, Julito. The boy's face reddened at the sudden attention.

"By now you have heard a lot about the massacre at Salta Tigre. As you know, esos cabrones wiped out an entire village. They have done it before, you know, but this time there is a difference. This time, se jodieron, they really fucked up killing the Franciscan priest — you know, an American. And that's the difference. The gringos are helping with helicopters and we're on their tails right now, practically in Honduras."

"Presidente, you know the opposition says it wasn't the guerrillas at all, that it was the Army."

"Pura mierda. Don't believe that political shit. There is absolutely no evidence of that."

"Presidente, even the U.S. State Department says there was no guerrilla activity near Salta Tigre. There still isn't any, and there aren't any media reports of any actions."

"You don't believe what you read in the papers, do you Mr. Jonas?" The president smiled.

"It's what I do, sir."

"Of course. I didn't mean that. I mean that there is a difference between reporting the truth and reality, the reality of what really goes on."

"No entiendo, presidente."

"The reality of Salta Tigre is that a village was wiped out, but the truth about Salta Tigre, the truth that you report, the truth I tell you, the truth they tell you, which you report truthfully according to fulano or mengano, is anybody's truth, and everybody's truth belongs to nobody, like a woman who sleeps with anybody. That truth is a whore."

"But that whore is still a woman."

"There's some truth to that," the president said and then laughed a high-pitched laugh.

When Harding wrote about the meeting later, he remembered that laugh, the laugh of a workingman in a cantina after a few drinks. It seemed to cut through a veneer, to expose the man. But Harding couldn't read the exposed man. The laugh was just out of place.

"And Ramírez..." Harding paused catching himself, sensing the moment, "I'd like your statement on the Ramírez killings. The whole family..."

"Please. Leave Ramírez out of this," the president snapped back and for the first time, Harding thought he saw a glimpse of the man's real temper. "I'm still in shock over those killings," he said. "That's my statement. My office is now handling the investigation. Look, you should go to Salta Tigre and see for yourself. I have a new commander there, Colonel Watson. You would be the first international journalist in there with Watson."

"Watson?"

"English name, but completely Central American like you." He smiled, just noticeably, at the surprise in Harding's eyes. The president had done his research. "British grandparents."

"I was planning to be back in Miami tonight."

"I thought you would want to go see Salta Tigre."

"I don't even have the right gear with me to go to the interior, and how would I arrange the trip?"

"The Air Force will fly you to Salta Tigre early tomorrow. I've already told Watson to take you to the village. It's something you need to see."

The President sipped his coffee. "Jonas," he said, pausing to let his use of the first name linger, "I would like to tell you something for your own background only, not for publication at this time." Harding almost said that this was an on-the-record interview when the president waved his hand. "O.K, O.K, don't worry," he said. "You can go with it now if you like. It's a good update on Salta Tigre, which is old news anyway." Harding knew immediately that the president was using him, was sure of it, but he also knew that if he followed along there would be a story.

"We have some new evidence of Cuban advisors supporting the guerrillas. If it's widespread, that would be a new escalation of the war, and that is disastrous for us at this time. The guerrillas drain our lifeblood, and we are still rebuilding from the earthquake. Go see Antigüa. It will make you cry."

"How many Cubans? Does Watson have any details on Cuban involvement?"

"The situation changes continually. The Americans spotted the latest incursion near Honduras. Watson will put you al día."

Harding left the presidential palace, went directly to the telex office and wired a short to Miami quoting the president on the new Cuban presence in Guatemala. He asked the national desk to try and confirm the story with State and notified Rosenfeld that he was traveling to Salta Tigre. Then he went to a bar near the Panamericano and tended to a bottle of La Negrita rum. Behind him, a Mayan maiden stripped down to a g-string danced awkwardly to a blaring rendition of "Macho Man." She came to his table and they finished the rum together. She placed her hand on his knee and worked it up to his crotch. He ordered another bottle.

He didn't want to see Salta Tigre. There was nothing there. He knew that, but he couldn't refuse the president's offer, and yet he couldn't shake an emptiness in his lungs, in his guts, punctuated by the president's falsetto laugh, a feeling that even the memory of Sally Beardsly's oranges-and-smoke-scented body was unable to fill. He thought of her sauntering happily through Mayan temples in Tikal, but Ramírez's bloody table-cloth surged to his mind.

He leaned on the sink in the cramped men's room, ran the water, slapping some on his face and looked up at a shaky image in a fading mirror, drunken tears welling to his surprise in an ebbing rum-driven blackness. What's the fucking difference, chico?

CHAPTER FOUR

Salta Tigre

"He really had been through death,
but he had returned
because he could not bear the solitude."
— GABRIEL GARCÍA MÁRQUEZ, *ONE HUNDRED YEARS OF SOLITUDE*

The patrol

Shortly after dawn, Harding was flying over mountains into a gray sky in a small single-engine trainer with tandem flight controls. The pilot pointed to the looming dark clouds and shook his head. Harding squirmed. *I don't want to know about it. Just get us there.* The young lieutenant didn't say much. He assumed the gringo spoke no Spanish. Once in a while he would look at a checklist and flip switches. Harding wished he hadn't seen the checklist. He would have preferred a pilot without a checklist. He would have preferred a good night's sleep instead of too much rum. The pilot pushed down on the yoke and Jonas felt the vacuum pull in his stomach and as the plane banked sharply to the left, his guts lifted into his throat. The small plane fell steeply, seeking only jungle, but then a thin strip of dirt appeared and widened and then they were bouncing on earth. He pushed the flimsy door open as the plane slowed to a stop, leaned over and puked.

––––––

Watson had watched the plane bank, find its bearings between the trees, then touch down on the muddy landing strip and bump along to a stop. He knew the pilot would have to return almost immediately to avoid the afternoon rainstorm already forming. He watched the gringo vomit and stagger out of the plane and he smiled to himself. Wearing a rumpled white suit, a white shirt open at the collar, a loosened tie, wingtips and a briefcase, the reporter looked completely unprepared to follow a combat patrol into the jungle. Welcome to Salta Tigre.

A Nikon dangled from Jonas's neck as he and Watson stood over a large table bearing mortar shell fragments and a heavy map crisscrossed with dark-red arrows. Watson noted that Jonas stood shaky and pale with an obvious hangover. The airstrip was ten kilometers south of Salta Tigre, near the Honduran border, Watson said, placing his .45 automatic pistol on one corner of the curling map. The arrows showed the village, the advance of the guerrillas and their probable exit and destination.

"They were gone when the Army arrived," he said, "right toward Honduras. But no reports that they crossed the border." He pointed to the Chinese markings on the mortars and other ordnance from the guerrilla attack that had decimated Salta Tigre.

"Any guerrilla activity since Salta Tigre?" Jonas said.

"It's been quiet," Watson said. "We believe they're concentrating in the south, with Cuban assistance. U.S. Intelligence reported more Chinese and Soviet ordnance and definite sightings of Cuban advisors."

"But why now? Why would the Cubans get into this shit now, when the Carter administration is their best bet since the Bay of Pigs to normalize relations and get rid of the embargo?"

"They don't want normal. They like revolution. That's their lifeblood. And it isn't just now. The Cubans have been around for a while. After the Bay of Pigs, they established a presence. Remember that Ché got his baptism of fire in Guatemala fighting for Árbenz."

"Yes, I know."

They stepped out of Watson's headquarters, a ranch house surrounded by military tents and vehicles and several groups of soldiers and rolled out of the encampment with six armed troopers in two Jeeps. A fine rain started, and the Jeeps disappeared into a jungle road, hitting every pothole. "We have a bit of a trek ahead of us," Watson said.

Taste the gun

On his back in the tall grass, Miguel played with an M-16, holding it up to the sky, sighting at the sun, and letting the rifle fall on his chest, twining his toes into the handle and the trigger guard and shining the gun with the palms of his hands. He preferred the weight and the smell of the stamped metal AK-47 María Osorio had given him. It wouldn't jam, and it smelled like a man, but the M-16 was a trophy won in an ambush, and he could always count on gathering ammunition from the Army. The gun warmed up from the handling, and he held it to his face and licked it, tasting the burned residue. Only a rifle that had seen a fight tasted that way, after firing it steadily, again and again, until at the burning point the gun's grease smoked. And now he was going home.

For a long time, Salta Tigre was all that Miguel, perhaps fifteen, but looking more like twelve, knew of the world until the guerrillas came and took him along, and then he discovered new towns and once even saw the capital. Some of the guerrilla leaders made speeches in a Spanish that he could hardly under-stand, but it didn't matter — he understood well enough with-out listening to anything. He lived in one of the small adobe huts huddled between the rainforest and the fence that surrounded the big plantation, and his life was made up of chickens, dogs, goats and corn grown on land that belonged to el patrón.

Sometimes el patrón and his men would come and take the corn to feed their cattle. Sometimes el patrón would threaten the villagers to come work for him or move on. They under-stood that it was his land and they had no legal right to farm it, but they also understood that they had to farm to eat and they didn't want to work for el patrón, who gave them only a little corn for their work — not enough to live on. They loved the hills that melted into the rain forest, near the graves of their ancestors, and they would never leave.

This time, though, the soldiers came and pulled the boys from their houses and shot them, one by one, and then the older men and the women and the small ones and the goats, the dogs and the chickens and then they burned the little houses and the bodies, leaving ashes and smoking stumps and black bones. Suddenly, Miguel sprang from the grass and sprayed bullets at a flapping flock of buzzards.

"No, no, Miguel, son nuestros amigos, hermanito." They're our friends, little brother. No more firing unless I tell you, understand? Ya no dispares más hasta que yo te diga, ¿men-tiendes?" María said

"Sí, María."

They were only half a day away from Salta Tigre now.

Returning to Guatemala after her final year of medical school in Havana, María Osorio, 38. had followed the river out of Honduras, northwest into the Guatemalan Mayan country, staying on the jungle paths near streams, as was her custom, hiking from village to village. Some of the young men, mostly just boys, and sometimes a young woman, would follow her, and she trained them to fight the hitanrun — a Central American education, she called it. She could work in the field only a few months and stay effective, and even so she returned to Havana emaciated and sick with constant dysentery, her nerves shot to hell, hecha mierda.

Go back to school, comandante Águila would say, we need more doctors, but then the call would come again and she would sit in Águila's office looking out the tiny window on Avenida de las Américas listening to the need and, yes, she would say, she would fulfill her commitment.

On this trip, Miguel was one of her first recruits, and hearing the boy tell the story of Salta Tigre she understood why the villagers turned away now when they saw her. On her first mission two years before, they'd received her with smiles and food and a corner in their homes for her sleeping bag. She treated their infections, abscesses and conjunctivitis, showing them how to make eyewash with boric acid and water, explaining to the mothers how diarrhea was a greater killer of children than bullets and how to give plenty of limeade sweetened with a little sugarcane juice to children when the diarrhea started.

Now, the villagers were quiet when she arrived, not responding with the usual familiar greetings. They still fed her, but she should move on, on to the next village, they said. They didn't want to know her. They didn't want to remember her. They had heard about the massacre at Salta Tigre and that was too close, for they knew the dead and knew that soldiers needed little cause. Now some hoped they would be left alone if only they did not help the guerrillas in any way, but her student guerrillas still followed her, knowing that ultimately the soldiers would come anyway, that there was no alternative, and she kept a dozen along the way, the oldest perhaps sixteen.

Moon Orchids

Colonel Watson and his men parked the two Jeeps under over-hanging leaves of banana trees growing on the last vestiges of a coffee plantation that melted into a steaming wilderness densely aromatic from a brief rainstorm in the early afternoon. The kidney-busting Jeep ride was over, and now they would hike up the mountain to Salta Tigre, about five kilometers. Watson pulled himself out of the Jeep and shrugged his massive shoulders, stretching. A broad, muscular man, he stood taller than Jonas's six feet and a full head above any of the troopers. He studied Jonas and knew that the reporter wasn't physically prepared or properly equipped for a five-kilometer hike up a jungle mountain.

"I thought we'd drive the Jeeps all the way up," Jonas said. Watson was giving instructions to his men and didn't hear. No one responded. Jonas dropped his jacket in the Jeep, but slung the camera around his neck and grabbed his briefcase

"You won't need that," Watson said.

"It's got my notebooks, tape recorder and film," Jonas said.

They started slowly, three men in front, Watson and Jonas in the middle, his camera dangling from his neck, and the rest of the troop behind them. Then the pace picked up. They splashed across a shallow stream and followed its contour for a while, the men walking in strong easy strides, smoking quietly.

His wet shoes heavier, clumsier, Jonas fell behind. Watson chain-smoked — lighting a cigarette with a clicking Zippo every hundred meters or so. The cigarette smoke and the smell of the lighter filled Jonas's lungs as he strained to keep up, the nausea returning, lunging into his throat. When the trees and foliage parted occasionally, the sun swept across his head like an open flame. He could feel blisters bubble on his feet, and he stopped for a moment, handing the briefcase to the nearest trooper.

Noticing Jonas's discomfort, Watson picked up the pace. The gringo was out of shape and his city clothing and wingtip shoes and what smelled like a hell of a hangover more than doubled the natural discomfort of climbing into the jungle. He knew Jonas had not bought the story on the Cuban. It was a fact that a Cuban had been spotted, but the only evidence Watson could offer was a sketchy intelligence report from the U.S. Southern Command. There was no physical proof. But what if the Cuban showed up here and now? Hell of a surprise. But Watson knew there was little chance of that, since the sighting was a hundred kilometers away and the Cuban probably wouldn't come this far west after Salta Tigre. But what if the Cuban were to show up in Salta Tigre, and the gringo died in a firefight? Gabriela was right. That would shift attention away from any Army involvement in the massacre and would fuel the outrage they needed to draw more dollars from Washington. Gabriela didn't have to say that much. The plan was clean-cut and totally plausible. He would have to produce that Cuban.

Watson talked to his men as he walked, pointing out animal tracks and a huge mahogany standing out in the tropical landscape. "You can build ten houses with that one," he said. The echoing response was always the same. "Sí, mi coronel. Sí, mi coronel."

The stream narrowed and the current strengthened, slapping white foam against the stones. Watson called a halt and sat on his haunches for a few minutes, smoking with his troops, motioning to a family of bright purple flowers sprouting out of crevices on the rocky embankment, spotlighted by an errant ray of sunlight.

"¿Qué belleza, verdad?" So beautiful.

Jonas heard the soldiers respond quietly as if not wanting to disturb the serene beauty of the flowers, "Sí, mi coronel, sí, mi coronel," and he envied their relationship, the camaraderie of soldiers in the field, something he remembered from his brief tour in Nam, but could never experience now in his lonely work. Out of shape and dehydrated from the hangover, the trek and the heat, he couldn't keep his breath and his heart had gone into palpitations, thumping uncontrollably even as he rested, as though rampantly searching for blood he didn't have to nourish a body abandoning him limb by limb as he slouched along behind the troops, shuffling, teetering on a tightrope. Watson offered his canteen and Jonas drained it. "Dicen que son guarias moradas," they say they're purple orchids, Watson said softly. No one moved. No one tried to touch the flowers as they leaned into the water, fresh and dripping after the rain as though newborn. "Pero de verdad son lunares, guarias lunares. ¿Saben qué son las lunares?" But they're really moon orchids. Know what moon orchids are? Watson said.

"No, mi coronel."

"Nadie las conoce. Son secretas." Nobody knows them. They're secret. Then louder, to Jonas, "They're moon orchids, little, tiny moon orchids. Seen them before?"

"No, sir."

"These orchids drink from the moon, night and day. In daylight, the sun shines so terribly hard it burns out the moon, but these orchids still drink from the invisible moon."

"Moon orchids," Jonas said

"Si las miran bien, verán que son un montón de florecitas chiquiticas arrejuntadas, no como las moradas, que son una sola. Y el jugo de la mata cura las cortaduras. No se olviden." If you look at them closely, you'll see they're a bunch of tiny little flowers, not a single flower like the purple ones, and the sap from the stem heals cuts. Don't forget.

"Sí, mi coronel. No son moradas."

"Son guarias lunares."

"Sí, mi coronel."

A small clearing appeared and two emaciated dogs rushed out barking from a thatched adobe hut with whitewashed walls painted blue along the ground. Watson talked to a short woman, all black hair and a plump white apron, about the weather, and it seemed he was singing an aria the way he waved his big hands and gazed at the sky, but he was only asking for lemons for the canteens, gesturing at Jonas.

"¿Hay limones?"

"No hay. Tengo naranjas." No lemons, oranges.

"Está bien."

She left for a moment and returned with a large burlap bag of oranges followed by a slight boy in a T-shirt and cut-off jeans that swung like bells below his knees. She shoved the bag at him.

"Ayúdelos, Miguel." she snapped at the boy and he joined the troops carrying the bag, which looked much larger in his arms, as they made their way up the mountain.

————

Crouching near the mound's summit María waited for Miguel to return with food. Then she saw the troopers approaching the hut. ¿Coño, de dónde salieron? Where the hell did they come from? She didn't think they'd be back so soon after burning down Salta Tigre. She didn't want a fight now. She wanted time to survey the area, calculate the risks.

She had a good view of the valley down to the little white and blue hut, up to the windblown trees that obscured her view now and then like shutters closing on a window. She adjusted the individual oculars on the Russian field glasses but couldn't get a clear view. Four, maybe eight, and she couldn't find Miguel in the moving foliage.

She knew that Miguel was acquainted with the woman and would wait there after the soldiers left. She worried about him, though: He was self-confident and had some experience, but he was really only a child, and he could easily show his hand. With four, Miguel could draw them easily into the grass and her boys could finish them quickly, without risk. Miguel would be prepared for that and knew María was watching. With eight, well, eight meant an all-out firefight — hard to control — unless they were very lucky.

Focusing the binoculars again through the trees, she saw the soldiers leave the area of the hut and start up the hill, into the trees, Miguel following them, carrying a large burlap bag. Carajo, we never planned for that, she though, but we can't sit this one out. If we run they'll chase us all the way to Honduras. If Miguel didn't manage to scamper away quickly enough, drawing them into a crossfire, then María would have to bring the ambush to them, regardless of how many soldiers were coming up the mountain. Suddenly the shuttering foliage opened long enough for her to count seven soldiers and a man in civilian clothes with a camera, a gringo by the look of him.

The priest

As they approached the summit, Watson waved and yelled, "Llegamos." Jonas squinted at the scene below as his arm swept the panorama pointing to the scorched patch of earth and blackened trees that once formed the village named after the mountain — Salta Tigre. He felt disembodied, only the thumping of his headlong heart holding him tenuously together as he slid quietly to the ground, leaning against a tree from where he could see a narrow path forming into a thin valley a hundred meters below, the tall grass and jungle foliage that had begun to devour the remains of Salta Tigre and beyond that, about half a kilometer away, a high conical mound covered in long, fluttering clumps of grass. He felt around for the Nikon but could not bear the thought of lifting his arms.

"Nothing left," Watson said. "Nearly a hundred, all ages, wiped out."

"But why?"

"Who knows? No reason. Terror has its own logic. They collaborated; they didn't collaborate."

Jonas watched Miguel's fingers plunge into the soft oranges, splitting them open, handing them to him quickly. Totally dehydrated, Jonas sucked on them thirstily, chewing the rind and spitting out the seeds. Watson and his men sat in the shade in a semicircle, about fifty meters away.

"Dame más," Jonas managed to blurt as the boy split open the oranges in a nonstop flow of sticky syrup. He couldn't get enough of the juice. "¿Cómo te llamás; de dónde sos?" What's your name; where are you from?

"Miguel, Padre," he said. Jonas could tell the boy was startled by the Spanish. "From here, from Salta Tigre. They're gonna kill us, Padre."

"¿Por qué decís eso?" Jonas challenged. He was a shy kid. He said he wondered at first if he should confide in a gringo, but he could confess to a priest, and he was sure the Army meant to kill them both. He said he knew the Americans were the enemy, as bad as the Army because they supplied the helicopters and the M-16s, but it was clear Jonas was a gringo priest like the other American priests and nuns that came to teach and like the one killed at Salta Tigre. For that reason, they meant to kill Jonas, and him too. There couldn't be any witnesses, he said. "You're a priest, and they kill the priests, the gringo priests."

Fear invaded the nausea in Jonas's stomach, draining any remaining strength from his body. He looked at Miguel, really seeing for the first time that he was diminutive, the size of a twelve-year-old but with the moustache fuzz of an adolescent and strong enough to carry the bag of oranges up the mountain. Who's gonna kill us? Why did he think I was a priest. Maybe the white shirt and tie. Hey, I'm not a priest, Jonas told him, but he was too tired to argue.

"Hey Miguel, I'm a journalist. There's no danger from guerrillas here."

"Not guerrillas, Padre, not guerrillas. The Army, the Army."

"But why, why?"

"Because they kill everyone."

"But not us. I'm not a priest."

"Doesn't matter, they always kill everybody."

"In Salta Tigre?"

"Yes, of course."

"How do you know?"

"I saw it all."

"But they didn't kill you."

"No, I hid in the cave."

Miguel pointed to his hiding place, the mound in the distance.

"Tell me, how did it happen?" He listened to Miguel's whispering voice — the Army killed the priest, the Army killed them all. He shook Jonas's arm now and then as he told the story, but it didn't matter — fatigue finally swept a dark green blanket softly over Jonas's eyes.

Miguel's hands were small and hard, and waking in the rainforest, Jonas thought they were butterflies on his face. "Padre, Padre. Despierte, despierte." He opened his eyes to the afternoon and focused on the mound in the distance, the tall grass blowing in an ebb and flow forming a pattern as it rippled, a pattern that left gaps, the outlines of stairs and doorways in the hill and he realized that Miguel's cave must be an ancient Mayan ruin now almost completely covered by foliage.

"Vamos, padre, vamos pa' la cueva. Vamos."

Miguel looked around as if wanting to see the troops, but not wanting them to see him looking. If the soldiers killed Jonas then, claro, he said, the soldiers would kill them both. Miguel was sure of that. There was no time left, he said.

"Padre, nos van a matar. Vamos, vamos." They're gonna kill us. Vamos.

Jonas blinked up at the small hands pulling on him and at the dark boy's serious, troubled face, and he stood up unsteadily, shaky on soaked blistered feet, and not then or ever knowing really why, perhaps to assuage the boy, but no longer an alien in this jungle, he hurried after Miguel, half stumbling down the mountain path.

"Corra, padre, corra, lo van a matar." Run, father, run, they're gonna kill you, Miguel hissed and he ran hoping the soldiers wouldn't notice for a few minutes and that they wouldn't fire at first or try to chase them down right away, giving them time to find some covering grass. Miguel pointed at the mound in the distance. "Vamos p'allá, la cueva."

———

Through the binoculars, María saw Miguel's tiny dark figure racing down the slope, sprinting toward her, darting for cover as he ran. She signaled the others to wait. Suddenly, a taller figure appeared behind Miguel, lumbering through the brush. María sighted him with the AK-47 but held back. She recognized the gringo. She signaled again to wait.

The temple mound

Watson and the troopers also kept Miguel, followed by Jonas, in sight as they scampered down the hill, toward the mound. Watson's raised hand pulled forward. "Vamos," he said, "con calma." He could have picked them off easily at that point, but there was no hurry. The gringo probably noticed the temple and the boy was guiding him to the ruins where the engagement already forming in his mind would take place, an event he wanted to choreograph carefully, building it with plenty of detail from this specific locale, detail that he would recall later consistently, realistically, and the boy completed the plan perfectly, providing the crucial missing element, the corpse of a guerrilla fighter.

"Ándele," he said.

The troopers, at a trot, fell into the same formation they had been following, three up front, Watson in the middle, followed by the other three.

———

María spotted the troopers jogging at a measured clip, about fifty meters behind the civilian, Miguel far ahead, nearing the temple. The soldiers maintaining that interval, not trying, it seemed, to gain on the gringo, were blundering headlong into her trap with no hint of caution, within range but without firing on the runners ahead. María knew that didn't make sense and for a moment she questioned the entire situation — was she falling into a trap? Possibly a helicopter? She held her breath and listened, scanning the skyline for a moment then with a "me cago en todo," fuck this, she stopped thinking and sighting on the biggest man, fired the first shot, giving the signal. The three troopers in back fell instantly as though yanked by the same rope while lingering blasts of gunfire brought down the three in front, one by one as they scattered.

———

Watson, hit in the groin, tore at the grenades on his shirt as he fell and unpinned them one by one lobbing them ahead one after the other at the brush near the temple mound. Crawling frantically into the foliage under the cover of the explosions, he collapsed, his face on the cutting grass, and, groping for his handgun, found the holster empty. He strained to quiet his breathing and lifted his head, scouring the brush, seeing nothing but weaving green between waves of darkness and then slowly, through the dripping leaves, the figure of a small man, no, a child, took form, sitting cross-legged on the ground before him like a shoeshine boy in the park pointing an AK-47 at his eyes.

———

The first explosion hit ahead of Jonas as he reached the temple mound, pounding his body, he would remember always, as the immense closed fist of an angry god, cracking a fissure in the earth under his feet and sucking him into the cavern like a baby, covering him in a shower of dirt and stones. The deafening force of a second and then a third explosion blasted around him, reverberating through underground rivers, deeply, eternally, sucking him into an angry ocean of slowly receding waves, gently lapping, and from an interminable distance, the diminishing surf whispered hoarsely, "No hay tiempo, no hay tiempo," no time, no time, and then louder, the tide returning, breaking frantically against him "Jale, jale. Coño, con cuidado, chico," pull, pull, carefully, as he broke through to the surface, gasping, an echoing surf, which turned out to be a woman shouting at his face, "Abra los ojos, chico." Open your eyes, chico.

———

Jonas looked like an earth-caked corpse as the guerrillas pulled him from the fissure into the fading afternoon light, coughing and snorting out dirt, his eyes shut in an eternal darkness. María lifted his chin and then stretching one eyelid open and then the other, poured saltwater into his eyes washing away the grime, loosening the contact lenses.

"Arde, verdá," burns, doesn't it, she said.

She peeled off the contact lenses and then with another liquid dripping from a plastic bottle rinsed his eyes and the open gash above his right eyebrow.

"Es agua bórica, para limpiar," she said. "No te preocupes, padre. Los lentes te salvaron la vista." It's a boric water eyewash. Don't worry father, the lenses saved your eyesight.

His sight blurred, eyes stinging, he focused nearsightedly on her hands as she worked on him and on the twisted scars on her left wrist and then on her face painted green and black swimming as she dripped the liquid into his eyes and finally on her blue eyes, brilliant behind the paint. She bandaged the gash above the right eyebrow, then lifted his arms and legs, testing the bones and the joints and put her hands inside his shirt feeling each rib.

"Todo enterito." You're whole, she said.

She ordered the boys to strip the soldiers, take the clothes and weapons and line the bodies up neatly along the front of the temple mound. Then, she gathered the young guerrillas, some of them now carrying two M-16s and everything the troopers had worn and waved them off, "Vámonos." Then, realizing Jonas could hardly hear, she put her face close to his and yelled, "Te vamos a dejar con la vieja. M'escuchas?" We'll leave you with la vieja. Can you hear me?

Jonas could only make out a blurry shadow in the waning afternoon as she faded away, striding with a slight limp. Squinting through the blur, he made out the bodies of Watson and his men, all seven of them on the ground in a neat row, six smaller brown forms and Watson's white mountain of a body and next to him Miguel's diminutive form wrapped in Watson's huge shirt.

"Antes de morir dijo que ereres padre, era creyente." He said you were a priest; he was a believer, María said, brushing the dirt off Miguel's face.

"Padre," she said, motioning to Jonas. Kneeling, Jonas made the sign of the cross, kissed his crossed fingers and gently placed them on Miguel's lips.

One of the boys took Jonas's arm and they began walking up the narrow valley. Looking around, wanting to remember, he looked back at the temple mound and at the ground below. The smoke had cleared; the dust had settled, silently revealing the waning afternoon. Two boys carried Miguel, his legs dangling from the shirt.

There is a clarity, he thought, *a clearing that can be achieved when time stops and you are in an ever-present moment and can sense forever, can smell every particle, hear every insect's breath and see sight itself as it moves about you meticulously, sensing it completely.*

The first zopilotes circled gracefully with full black wingspans tipped in white, some alighting in hesitant steps and then others pushing, crowding against each other more forcefully. When he reached the edge of the clearing and looked back again, he saw only roiling black in the dusk.

They're moon orchids.

CHAPTER FIVE

Mate en Dos

Chess is a war over the board.
The object is to crush the opponent's mind.
— BOBBY FISCHER

La vieja de las naranjas

Oranges, he thought. It's the old lady with the oranges. La vieja stood in the frame of the doorway, leaning her right shoulder on the doorjamb, her back to him, the back of her left wrist on her waist, the hand open toward him, the fingers stretching out and then curling in telltale little spasms. He lay near the door of the hut where the guerrillas had left him, eyes still gritty with dirt. He could feel that his face had puffed up. The explosions still reverberated in his head and blood dripped from his nose. Any movement hurt as he fell into a doze only to awaken choking on blood. Hurrying green Army uniforms and voices shouted questions at him. He answered, but they didn't hear. They asked in English fragments and he answered in Spanish, but they didn't understand, as though their minds refused to accept Spanish spoken by a gringo, so he switched to English. "My eyes," he said. One of them peered closely shinning a flashlight at his eyes and wrapped gauze over them, around his head. Then he felt a jab in his thigh, *must be morphine*, and he fell into delicious slumber, jostling into reality now and then to see himself transported in a criss-cross of headlights almost as a different body, by Jeep, then by helicopter and finally to a hospital emergency room in Guatemala City.

His nose was plugged up to stop the bleeding and he was breathing through chapped, cracked lips. Once in a while, he had to spit out a blood clot. A nurse poured something in his eyes and stitched the gash over his right eye. Then the doctor appeared in a tuxedo with a ruffled shirt and a red cummerbund. The nurse jammed Jonas's face into a wire frame that held his head immobile. The doctor moved in, alcohol on his breath, and pried open his eyes, delicately picking out debris with steel tweezers, a slight tremor in the hand. Jonas tried to name the alcohol, leaning toward La Negrita rum, but then figured that Johnny Walker Black was more appropriate to the tuxedo.

A day later he still hurt and couldn't see through the bandages. He noticed that his right arm was slow to lift and weak to reach as he fumbled for the water glass on the tray near his bed. The clean sheets of the hospital bed felt rich and smooth and his nose was unplugged and wasn't bleeding and the smell of Clorox was comforting. Later that smell mixed with the various nurse smells and when the bandages came off for eye drops he could tell that he wasn't completely blind and in two days could see well enough out of the right eye.

The other one would take some time, the doctor said. There had been a partial retinal detachment in the left eye, he said, corneal abrasions in the right.

"It's happened before," Jonas said.

"How?"

"Vietnam."

"Trauma — I hate trauma." He shrugged. "You want to go to the Bascom eye center in Miami when you get home, right away."

Now he could see the bruised face in the mirror, the funny thick eyeglasses he never used cockeyed over the bandaged left eye creating the walleyed look of a bewildered fish, the left cheek and that side of his forehead spattered with red pock-marks as if shotgunned. His cheekbones were swollen purple and his right eyebrow was stitched. He was getting around and pissing on his own and starting to think, and for the first time he paid attention to the Mayan, a little man sitting in a corner in front of a chessboard, slightly hidden by the curtain that divided the room. He wore a double-breasted brown suit with yellow pinstripes, a white shirt, starched collar, a black necktie pasted to a formidable double Windsor, square-toed black English oxfords and no socks.

"¿Usted quién es?"

"Vargas," he said, "de Presidencia," from the president's office.

"¿Para qué?"

"Para protegerlo," for protection. That's all he said, all he would ever say.

"You have a telex, Mr. Jonas," the nurse said. "Would you like me to read it?"

"Please."

"It's from a Rosy in Miami," she said in schoolbook English, and smiled. She wouldn't smile if she could see Rosy, two hundred pounds of gristle and tufts of bristles on the backs of his hands.

"Jonas," she read, "We're all pulling for you here. Hospital said you were recovering O.K. I can come get you if you think it necessary. Guatemalan president's office insisted on paying the hospital. Told them we cannot accept and will wire full payment. Please restate that when possible. When you can, please call. I'd like to put together a story. You dictate. We'll write it here. Relax. Don't worry about returning right away unless you want to. Regards, Rosy." The nurse pulled the blinds down and darkness enveloped him in layers.

The idea of talking with Rosy provoked nausea, a sort of hangover nausea that lingered without vomit. Trying to make sense of his situation and the events of the past few days was debilitating. He couldn't hold it, couldn't contain it in one story, like pulling on lianas hanging in the jungle, hanging everywhere but insufficient. Any way he looked at it, it was distorted. The murder of the Ramírez family was a terrifying recurring flashback. Watson steered him into an ambush and buried him alive like a sacrifice to the Mayan gods. The anger and fear that enveloped him could not be wrapped up in newsprint. Any story would be an insufficient lie, and he couldn't write that story. Maybe all stories were insufficient lies, and he was a liar in his sullen craft.

He awoke inside his childhood letting himself hover there, knowing he wasn't a child again and was awake and in a hospital in Guatemala, but he let go, lingering in the twilight memory of Macedonio's crystal cave on Abuelo's farm near the Reventazón River, and then the river rapids became a rumbling in his head and a terror in his guts. The fear was connected to his childhood now, he thought, only because of Salta Tigre. Falling into that pit in the Guatemalan jungle had somehow revived an old image that came back through the blur of his eyes and the ringing in his head. It's the image of Carlitos' door, but it feels like Salta Tigre.

The door is important. He saw the door from the inside. He's already inside and Carlitos has pulled his pants down around his legs so he can't run. Behind them, a quiet figure sits strapped into a child's highchair and moves a little. But it's dark, and he can't see well that far anyway. Now he's on his stomach, face pressed against the wood floor. The door cracks open a little and he can see dust blow with his breath. Carlitos is heavy on top of him.

Abuelo would come to get him that summer and would tell his favorite story.

His grandfather's story was always the same story, told in chapters and at the end of all the chapters Jonas would say, "Tell it again, Abuelo," and he would. Jonas couldn't remember now what was story and what was real. Perhaps the story had nothing to do with life. Perhaps the story was all story and just story. Even without the story, however, he remembered hugging his grandfather and the old man's goodnight kiss, burning his cheeks with his rough stubble and Jonas tracing the path of the bullet, no wider than a finger, from his forehead to the temple, up to the rough part above the ear where it had stayed until Macedonio sucked it out.

And the old man told the story, the orange pack of Tico cigarettes, the blue smoke, tobacco stains on his hard fingernails. That memory was real, and so was Salta Tigre lighting fear at the core of his heart, a dark hard fear.

Salta Tigre was like an earthquake that lasted only moments, but continued to generate aftershocks that cracked the earth around him into a network of fine chasms, releasing troublesome little demon bubbles of ancient guilt, guilt with-out detectable origin, guilt that had somehow freed itself from any identifiable source, yet continued to float to mind as mutant creatures surfacing from an underground sea. He cried then for Ramírez and them all, the dead and the living too. He thought no soy yo, no soy yo, and he thought, but you, Jonas, you are hijo de algo, and he thought of Zulema turning, of her hands plunging into the sackcloth bag, sifting, lifting the red-ripe coffee berries and letting them spill through her cut and swollen fingers. Hijo de algo and he thought of his father's sputtering plane plunging into the Reventazón River Valley, plunging toward the beginning of Jonas's life. Hijo de algo and he thought of Julia, young and beautiful, turning as she did, her left hand upturned at the wrist, hazel-green eyes catching light, plunging into darkness. Hijo de algo, and turning he thought of Abuelo, plunging into the black-green rainforest canopy. Hijo de algo and he thought of Chevo's machete flashing and the man's arm, severed, falling. And he thought of uncle Hans, turning to glance at him as the bow of his cello sang smoothly on the strings. No soy yo, no soy yo, he thought, a voiceless confirmation that it couldn't be him there before that horror, but another man who also would be the one responsible, *because it was not my fault, not my fault,* but he felt guilt plunging into his chest, leaving it empty as a black hole, lungs like vacuums suffering a terrible embrace. No soy yo, no soy yo. It was the same cry he heard when he saw the Ramírez family — it's not me, it's not me — but now he realized that that was a different cry, and the difference was that in his mind, it was always in Spanish, and in Spanish it really meant, I am not me, I am not me. And, turning, he saw Ramírez, his smile flashing white in the tanned face. And he thought of that sea creature that invades his dreams, with new tendrils floating, searching, a phantom sea maenad nourishing herself from microscopic ambient life that bliss-fully floats by only to fatally adhere to the creature's nearly invisible filaments. It's not me; it's not me, he thought. A door cracks open a little and on his stomach, face pressed against the wood floor. he can see dust blow with his breath. Carlitos is heavy on top of him and then turning, he thought of Macedonio's crystal hideaway, tucked in his heart, hijo de algo, hijo de todo.

That was the summer Abuelo would come to get him. They would pal around that summer and he would tell his favorite story. His grandfather's story was always the same story, told in chapters and at the end of all the chapters Jonas would say, "Tell it again, Abuelo," and he would. Jonas couldn't remember now what was story and what was real. Perhaps the story had nothing to do with life. Perhaps the story was all story and just story. Even without the story, however, he remembered hugging his grandfather and the old man's goodnight kiss, burning his cheeks with his rough stubble and Jonas tracing the path of the bullet, no wider than a finger, from his forehead to the temple, up to the rough part above the ear where it had stayed until Macedonio sucked it out.

And the old man told the story, the orange pack of Tico cigarettes, the blue smoke, tobacco stains on his hard fingernails. That memory was real, and so was Salta Tigre lighting fear at the core of his heart, a dark hard fear.

Jonas lumbered to the bathroom. The face faintly fluttering back at him looked more, with time, like his grandfather, an old man, older somehow than all old men, not wiser perhaps, but more wounded, tougher.

Havana

María didn't know why an Army colonel had foolishly crossed her path at Salta Tigre, but she knew he would be missed by morning and her guerrillas had to disappear into the jungle quickly, traveling fast, as fast as they could, covering their tracks.

After a half-day's march through coffee fields and jungle, she ordered the boys to wrap their weapons in the soldiers' uniforms. They buried everything, leaving it well marked near a clearing, and then they swung southeast toward the Honduran border. The boys peeled away from the column quietly, one by one, as they passed each village, leaving all trace of the fire-fight behind.

Finally, she was alone.

She dug a hole, stripped and buried all her clothes, gear and weapons, keeping only a black nun's habit and a straw hat. American nuns had been working on the Honduran side for years, and with her blue eyes and good English she always passed. She checked for the sewn pouch inside the habit and felt the hidden packet. She ripped the stitches and fished out a plastic bag holding a map, compass, U.S. passport, several hundred dollars in U.S. and Honduran currency and a long flat key. She placed the brass compass on the map and calculated the time she needed to reach the Honduran border. Then she started the long hike through the brush. Her one great advantage, she knew from previous missions, was her gender. They would be looking for a man.

Once in Honduras, she found her way to Santa María de Verduras, a town just big enough for her to fall into place without much notice, checked into a posada and slept for almost two days. Awakening, she felt pain over most of her body and for a few minutes was unable to stand. She recovered slowly, venturing out after a few hours for a restaurant meal, and sitting in the central plaza in front of the church, she nodded at the passers-by who acknowledged the nun's presence. The Tegucigalpa newspaper said that the Honduran military was cooperating with the Guatemalan government's search for the guerrillas responsible for ambushing an Army patrol and assassinating the Army chief of staff. The group was believed to be, the article said, the same one that a month earlier had massacred the inhabitants of Salta Tigre and burned down the village. The story said that an American journalist had survived the attack. The priest, she smiled.

The next day, she boarded a bus to San Pedro Sula and once there went directly to the downtown office of the Banco Anglo Americano and followed a sprightly bank teller to the safe deposit boxes.

The clerk inserted a key into one of the boxes and María inserted her key and turned it. The clerk turned her key and pulled out the box. "Tome, madre," she said, examining María's tired face.

"Gracias, corazón," she said, turning away from the young woman. Exactly as she expected, the box contained ten thousand U.S. dollars in $100 bills and some Honduran currency, an Iberia Airline ticket to Santo Domingo and a 9mm Beretta with two loaded clips. She took the Honduran cash and the ticket and returned the box to its niche, then went next door to the Iberia office.

A week later she was in Havana.

End Game

After a week in the hospital Jonas was restless, suffocating and longing to get out. The bruises had stopped hurting, and the cuts and scratches were healing nicely. His head still rang, revving now and then like a loaded truck straining up a hill in first gear. One eye was still taped up, the other one oversensitive to light and hard to focus. Without contact lenses, he had to wear the old eyeglasses taped against the bandage. His right arm, now in a sling, was useless. sat near the curtain playing chess from a book, studying the moves, holding the pieces as if trying to guess their weight before pushing them along. He never invited Jonas to play. As he lay in bed trying to focus his right eye, Jonas stared at the Indian's sockless ankles sticking out from the pinstriped pants.

"Is there a Bobby Fischer game in that book?"

Vargas didn't answer. Then, "No hablo inglés."

They had reduced Jonas's morphine to next to nothing, and he began to feel a familiar craving that crept out of his stomach leaving an emptiness that only alcohol could fill. He stretched out an arm waving a $20 bill.

"Oiga, Vargas. Cómpreme una botella de ron Negrita, por favor," buy me a bottle of Negrita rum, please.

Vargas's eyes didn't move from the chessboard. "No puedo salir," I can't go out, he said, finally.

"Bueno, carajo, juguemos. Si le gano, me compra el ron," O.K., fuck it, let's play. If I win, you buy me the rum, Jonas said.

"Stá bien," Vargas said, sticking out his fists. Jonas picked the left one. Black. Vargas pushed his king pawn up two.

Jonas tapped the black king pawn forward to meet his. "¿Trabajás para Rosales, verdad?" You work for Rosales, right? He could see Vargas's mind shifting away from chess.

"No." His queen pawn moved up one, looking for the fool's mate. "Trabajo para presidencia." I work for the president's office.

Jonas blocked the mate, and they went into the middle game. He could tell Vargas was disappointed.

"Mate en dos," mate in two, Jonas said.

"De todos modos, no puedo salir." Anyway, I can't go out, Vargas said.

Then Jonas played his favorite gambit. He told Vargas that they could trade sides and Jonas could still checkmate him in less than ten moves.

"Ni mierda," Vargas said, as Jonas mated him.

"Comprá dos. Una pa mí, una pa ti." Buy one for me and one for you, Jonas said switching to the familiar and smiled at him in what must have been a hideous grimace, because Vargas shot up, snatched the bill and disappeared.

His belly warming with rum, Jonas reached for the stack of yellow telexes from Rosy, who was getting a bit shrill, not for him to get back, just for him to call. The paper needed a story from its own reporter, even if that meant interviewing its own reporter. "We'll put it together. Why won't you call?" he said in the last telex. In truth, Jonas didn't really know why he didn't call. But he felt strongly that he shouldn't call Rosy. Maybe because he was paid to be the storyteller, and now he couldn't tell the story. I don't own the story, he thought, the story goes so far beyond the story that it could never be told in a newspaper. It was as if his words had been ripped away as he fell from a clean place of safety, of antiseptic verbs and nouns and plastic gray-blue airplane cabins, plummeting through Ramírez's murder and Salta Tigre and through the creatures that lived in that undersea remembrance and into the dripping greenery of his childhood, and in that restless fall heard an echoing "fuck you," and it was his own voice still clinging above, trailing along, opening behind him like a parachute. He couldn't tell without words. And that "fuck you" held him aloft, lowering him half blind, ears still ringing, slowly down, gently. If he were to call Rosy, he would only whisper, "Fuck you, Rosy."

Now, as the rumbling in his head accelerated and the right eye tried to focus on Vargas's naked ankles, something came to him. It was nameless, formless, but it was something. He found all his gear neatly stacked in the closet, including the Nikon and the briefcase he'd carried in Salta Tigre. He searched his notes, not knowing exactly what he was looking for, until he came to the shoeshine boy's Tico Times. There it was. The article on the attempt on Ramírez's life and the photo showing Ramírez sitting on his living room sofa, his left arm in a sling and three bodyguards standing nearby, one of them with an expressionless Mayan face, wearing a dark suit, the pants hanging too high above sockless ankles and square-toed black oxfords.

He called Pan Am and made a reservation for a late afternoon flight to Miami. Vargas heard. It couldn't be helped. Jonas grabbed some clothes and put them on in the bathroom, hoping to slip out quietly. When he opened the door, Vargas was there holding the phone. It was Rosales.

"Chico," he said, "you're in no shape to travel."

"They want me in Miami," Jonas said.

"You can't even see," Rosales said.

"It's not that bad."

"We feel responsible," he said. "Vargas will go with you, all the way to Miami."

"I don't need him."

"You can hardly see."

"O.K."

"Don't worry about the hospital. We already covered it," Rosales said. Jonas remembered Rosy's insistence on covering the bill, but he let it go. Fuck it.

Jonas finished off the rest of the rum and told Vargas to bring his stuff and meet him in the lobby. He hurried down and hailed a cab. He wasn't about to get into a car with the little prick.

As he approached the Pan Am counter, he saw Vargas following him with the bag. He got both tickets and handed them to him.

"Espéreme aquí. Voy al baño." Wait for me here, I'm going to the john, he said.

He went around a corner, in and out of the men's room, into a teeming crowd of tourists clamoring for passage to

Tikal, then straight to the Lacsa desk.

"One way to San José," he said. "When's the next flight?"

"In two hours," she said.

"Too long. Can you check with Tan or Copa?"

She tapped the keys. There's a Taca flight leaving in ten minutes," she said. "Corra."

Vargas had all his stuff, notes and film, but so what, he thought, if you're dead you don't need anything anyway.

CHAPTER SIX

The Crystal Cave

He was a handsome man
and what i want to know is
how do you like your blue-eyed boy,
Mister Death.
— BUFFALO BILL'S DEFUNCT, E. E. CUMMINGS

The pilot

The mechanic gave the P-39 Aircobra a thump on the muzzle,
and the pilot switched on the ignition. Twelve cylinders behind
his back coughed and shuddered into a vibration frenzy,
traveling forward through the driveshaft under his scrotum,
snapping the prop into a whiz and then the airstrip at Limón
was just a sliver of black as he headed off, into the rising sun,
toward the Caribbean looking for German submarines.

The young man's shoulders almost touched the sides of the
cockpit and his knees jammed into the instrument panel.
He looped south and fell into the usual daydream, cherry
blossoms on the Tidal Basin and a brown-haired girl in the
pedal boat, and he laughing to himself as he tried to explain
to his mother in Yiddish what the Panama Canal was and

what Hitler wanted with a little Central American country named Costa Rica.

He spotted no submarine shadows or periscopes parting the waters on that mission, and he banked away from the horizon back to the coast, looping a ribbon past Limón, toward the mountains that ring San José for a view above the Irazú Volcano before landing at la Sabana Airport. It was clear and too early for the afternoon showers to sweep inland. He strained the plane to 17,000 feet, reaching a point over Irazú from where he could see both oceans.

Then the prop sputtered and stopped.

Oil pressure was O.K. He tapped the gauge. He had plenty of gas. The RPMs were revving right, and the huge engine was roaring but the electric prop went into erratic stalls and spurts for no reason, and he lost airspeed and altitude. He should have thought of bailing out immediately, but he'd used up his time fumbling with switches, hoping the prop would fully reengage.

He turned back toward Limón, just clearing Irazú, which shined golden at 10,000 feet, and he knew it would take too long to jump and survive the bailout, so he stayed with the plane. As he aimed it toward Limón, away from Irazú, he spotted the snaking Reventazón River near Turrialba.

He fell fast into the river valley and what looked like an open field. Almost in a stall, the nose down as tight as he could hold it, the plane plowed into a cornfield, cornstalks lashing the fuselage. He lost consciousness as the Aircobra jammed into the earth, tipping up against a cypress tree on the edge of a coffee plantation.

Mr. Death

Chevo answered the knock.

"Carajo, ¿qué te pasó?" What happened to you, he said, pulling Jonas up onto the plywood floor of the shack and touching his forehead gently.

"Salta Tigre me pasó," Jonas said.

"Contame," Chevo said. His strength felt comforting as Jonas told the story of Salta Tigre. Chevo smiled his wide grin, dimples like parentheses around the black Don Ameche moustache driving out all the old resentment Jonas had built up. Now the old man was family, family when he really needed it.

Chevo's shack looked barren and dusty, and Chucha was gone for good. The calico curtain had ripped some, and he could see the unmade bed.

"We should pay Tía Rosita a little visit in Turrialba," Chevo said. Now that Chucha was gone, he could go back home.

"¿Cuándo?"

"Ahora," he said.

"I'll go get us some beer," Jonas said.

"¿Puede ver bien?"

"Claro, no se preocupe," Jonas said, but he couldn't see well. The left eye was a blur and the right eye still burned, and his head was ringing as he walked away from Chevo's little house and looked up for the old fortress. He walked over to La Soledad, past his grandfather's old house to Carlitos's row-house, right up close to the door this time so he could see the wood grain, but he didn't knock. A sudden weakness took his breath away.

He went back slowly past La Soledad Cathedral and the gigantic cypress trees, and up to the Parque Central and bought four Imperiales at La Lora. He found Chevo sitting on the front step and he dropped down beside him.

"Está sudando a mares. You've been doing some work."

"Yes. Dame la Imperial."

"Working on the corn?"

"You have a visitor."

"¿Dónde?"

"Detrás, with the corn."

Chevo got up grabbed an Imperial and went inside. He popped off the bottle cap on the edge of the table. Jonas followed him through the room and stumbled over his own briefcase.

Vargas.

"¿Vargas?" Chevo said.

From the back door, he could see the little man outstretched on the ground next to a neat row of six uprooted corn stalks. He looked perfect in his brown pin-striped suit, very much as he always did in life, poker-faced, the brown skin smooth and glossy except for a puckering hole in the center of his forehead and two strings of blood trickling from his nostrils. Next to him, lined up with the corn plants, were a mini-Uzi with three extra clips, a big blue-black Smith and Wesson in a tan leather holster and three large folding knives.

"Grab a beer," Chevo said.

They sat quietly for a while on the backstep, sipping Imperial from the bottles and looking at Vargas. Chevo pulled out an orange and blue pack of Tico cigarettes and lit one. Jonas's vision blurred, making Vargas float. He thought of Ramírez and wondered at the simple irony that he should lead Vargas to the one place, the unexpected place, where

94

the bullet waited. He could see Vargas sizing up the old man, the little shack, the easy kill. And in the drawer of the worn desk, the smithanwesson twitched.

"He said he was delivering your bag. He came in, and as he sat down in front of me at the desk, I saw a piece of the Uzi under his jacket. At that moment, I looked at his eyes and saw that he meant to kill you and me too."

"You could see that?"

"Well, the Uzi was enough, wasn't it? But it was really the Indian blood. The blood speaks on its own to its own."

"What Indian blood? We have Spanish and Jewish and now...Indian?"

"Claro, your great-grandmother, Liquita. Where do you think Macedonio came from?

"I don't know. Was he family?"

"Blood speaks to blood without wanting, without talking. He thought his straight face would hide his intent. But I saw the killing in his eyes. So I thought fast, very fast, before he could read me, and I kicked the desk forward jamming him against the wall, pulled out the smithanwesson from the drawer and dropped him right there."

"Jesus."

They scraped a trench and placed Vargas neatly into it, folding his hands over his chest and smoothed down his coat. The earth settled on him almost like a natural part of his outfit. Chevo tore down the curtain that separated his bed from the desk, ripped it into strips, soaked them in water and wrapped the roots of the corn stalks. He dropped the Uzi, the pistol and the knives into a paper bag. "Vámonos," he said

"¿Adónde?"

"To see Rosita in Las Pavas."

He lifted his beer. Looked for a second at the label's black Fascist eagle emblazoned on a background of gold. "Imperial, la mejor. Here's to culo y tetas," he said. "Los buenos vivos y los malos muertos."

"I'll get a taxi," Jonas said.

"It's a four-hour ride to Turrialba," Chevo said.

He looked at Jonas long, his soft brown eyes crinkling as he chugged the beer. They crinkled at the corn plants with their roots wrapped in calico, the dead little assassin, the grave. It all blurred together in Jonas's mind. Then he realized that Vargas was the one who murdered Ramírez and his family. He didn't know, but he knew. Maybe it was that Indian thing. "Let's bury the jueputa," he said.

Chevo dropped the empty bottle on Vargas's chest and palled down the grave. He gathered some clothes and wrapped them in the remains of the curtain. He unscrewed the hanging light bulb and placed it in the bundle. Jonas looked back as the taxi drove away. Nothing meaningful was left, just Vargas resting underground, behind a plywood lean-to with a tin roof.

Víboras

Chevo finished the beers, and they stopped in Cartago for a case, and Chevo started singing tangos written by his old pal Carlos Gardel. "Carlos, ¿no lo conoce?" He opened the window and let the moist wind hit him as he sang. Then he shifted to a Mariachi version of "La Feria de Las Flores," and when he got to the part about picking the most beautiful flower, tears flowed with the wind on his face.

As they rolled onto Turrialba's potholed main street an hour later, the cab driver honked at a line of half a dozen green taxicabs in front of El Caballo Blanco. When the drivers spotted Chevo, resonant in the last lines of his song, one by one they slammed into their cabs and burned rubber.

"¿Qué carajo les pasa?" the driver said.

"Tienen que cagar," Chevo said.

"¿Cómo?"

"Del miedo," Chevo said. They shit in their pants when they see him. "Ya no joden a Rosita," Chevo said. His 70-year-old hermanita was now safe from the cab drivers.

Rosita had married Efraín González, a farmer with land-holdings on the way to Limón. He started out managing the Álvarez farm in Las Pavas, outside of Turrialba, then later bought his own place and made plenty of money growing bananas for United Fruit. Efraín grew up with Chevo and went to the same Catholic school, La Salle, run by Jesuits. Chevo couldn't remember the details of the courtship, but he recalled the break-up vividly.

The marriage lasted only one twenty-four-hour period.

They got married at the home place in Las Pavas one afternoon, he said, and the next day they were going to Limón and then by steamer to New York — Abuelo's present. But the next morning Efraín appeared for breakfast with a swollen face, one of his teeth knocked out. Abuelo asked Efraín what happened, holding his chin, examining the swelling. "Su hija me dió, Don José Joaquín." Your daughter hit me, Don José Joaquín, Efraín said and he left. The family didn't know it then, but Efraín would never return to Las Pavas to manage Abuelo's coffee fields.

The kids called Efraín el Martillo in school, Chevo said. Efraín had the longest dick in school. No need to measure. Nobody even came close to a dick like that, down to the knees. And Efraín liked to play jokes with it. Chevo would be sitting in class and suddenly he's seen the thing resting there next to his arm, ready to strike. The cabecita wasn't like the head of your ordinary dick. It was shaped funny, like a hammerhead, like a baby hammerhead shark. It would scare the shit out of Chevo, and Efraín would howl. Well, later after Rosita kicked him out, Efraín got drunk with Chevo at the Caballo and he told the whole story. Turns out his dick wasn't only long, but when it got hard the damned thing would also swell up so big around that the fingers of a woman's hand couldn't go around it, and he never got it all the way into a woman. Only the funny head would ever fit. He just scared poor Rosita out of her wits. When she saw that thing, she swung at it with a shoe and then knocked the crap out of Efraín. Well, after that Rosita hated all men, "víboras," she called them. As she got older and stooped-over and funny looking, the Turrialba kids would torment her yelling after her, "Codorniz, codorniz, con un grano en la nariz y en el culo una lombriz." Then the taxi drivers started the same jodienda so she was afraid to go to market. The farm is a good ten kilometers from town, and she depended on the taxis. So she called Chevo and when he came around to see what he could do, he decided to have a little chat with the drivers. He went to el Caballo Blanco —Fritz owns it now — and sat near the door, sipping Imperial, watching the drivers go in and out. He knew them all. All local boys. Around noon, they gathered at el Caballo for lunch, and then they moseyed on over to the dispatcher's office for a smoke. So he bought a case of beer and took it over to the office. They got into the little office, about a dozen all together and started popping the beers.

¿Dónde está el jefe? Chevo said. The dispatcher stood up, and Chevo gave him a beer. Then Chevo kicked the door shut and pulled out the smithanwesson and said without raising his voice, Cabrones, ahora sí. Nobody gets out of here alive. They shut up. It was quiet as a cemetery as they stared at the revolver. You know that little lady, la Niña Rosita? Chevo said, The one you've been jodiendo? Well, she's my little sister, and now she's scared to go to the market, and I'm her big brother and I can't let that happen, so I'm gonna kill all you motherfuckers. Nobody gets out alive. Get on your knees, cabrones. They didn't move. They cried and started to make excuses. Chevo fired one shot into the ceiling and they dropped to their knees like somebody whacked off their legs with a machete, pissing in their pants. He grabbed el jefe and put the gun in his mouth. You gonna stop jodiendo Rosita, cabrón? And el jefe swore he would.

"All you jueputas gonna back off my hermanita?"

"Sí, sí."

"Lemme hear it loud, comemierdas," he barked at them, and they screamed, "Sí, sí, sí."

"Don't forget, motherfuckers," he said, and they didn't. Rosita never paid cab fare again.

Chevo lifted his bottle of Imperial in a brindis. The black eagle on a background of gold gleamed as he said, "Los tontos muertos y los vivos vivos. Culo y tetas, mijo, that's all that's worth a goddamn in this fucking life, en este miserable valle de lágrimas."

Mi casa es su casa

Las Pavas was beyond the Río Rojo creek, ten kilometers from Turrialba in the foothills of the rainforest mountains. Around Turrialba the hills started as coffee and bananas, rising toward the rain forest. Abuelo usually worked legal cases on a pay-as-you-can basis, so rich clients paid more, and one had paid with the farm early in the century, and the family summered there, away from bustling San José. Las Pavas was crisscrossed with winding crevices and canyons that dropped hundreds of feet, all leading to the Reventazón River, a real river twisting and breaking into whitewater as it coursed through the farm. As a kid, Jonas fished for bobos in the rapids — no rods, just nylon line with hooks dangling, snaring the fish in the rocks. The bobos had perky little shark noses, and the white meat was good eating when Zulema fried them fresh.

Rosita came out wiping her hands on a white apron as they drove up, hugged Jonas and then leaned back looking at his face. "Válgame Dios," she said, passing her hand over the bandage and the bruises and kissing him on the forehead. She glanced at Chevo but didn't approach him. "Chucha's inside," she said without looking at him.

"No me diga," Chevo said.

"¿Puedes ver?" she asked him, ignoring Chevo.

"Yes, I can see O.K."

She looked at him steadily, still holding his face. "You can't see anything, you never could and now —"

"You're right. No veo ni mierda."

"No me hable cochinadas," she said, mad at the shit word. He leaned forward and kissed her. With Rosita, you had to observe convention and good manners and all details of la buena educación, good breeding, or you were in mierda.

As they unloaded the taxi, he heard his uncle Hans' cello somewhere behind the house and the old familiar deep molasses notes of the instrument enveloping the house and the yard and wafting up through the coffee fields into the haze that descended from the high forests bringing the afternoon rain.

He went to the back porch and sat a little to the side. Hans caught him with the tail of an eye and turned slightly to look at him without interrupting the flow of his music and nodded, blue eyes smiling. Hans was in his sixties now, but like Chevo he looked robust, his gray-blond hair, combed back straight and severe, glistened in the afternoon light. He finished the piece slowly and sat quietly looking at the horizon a moment, then rose for the abrazo. "You remember the song?" he said. He spoke English with a British accent.

"Claro. You always played that piece for Abuelo.

"Always before sunset with some *ron colorado*."

"But I can't remember the name."

"Bruch's adagio of Hebrew songs, Kol Nidrei."

"That's for Passover, isn't it?"

"Yes, 'All Vows.' Bruch liked folk melodies and he heard a Jewish friend, a rabbi, sing Kol Nidrei at Passover. But it goes beyond that. In it you can hear all the blood of the Jewish people, you can see the creation and the dissolution and glimpses of pain, just glimpses, because it's adagio and deliberately boiled down, reduced to the essential flow, heavy flow. I heard Casals play it in London in '36 and loved it. Your grandfather also loved it, maybe because he was fond of the Jewish connection, but I think he just loved it."

"I never understood his Jewish connection."

"Well, there was your father, of course, but long before that the family had a Jewish connection. He said it was the Álvarez blood, Sephardic." Hans looked quietly at the younger man.

"Looks like you took a beating. What's wrong with your eyes?"

"I'm not blind. That's the best I can say. A grenade exploded near me in Guatemala. I was blinded by the shock of the explosion and flying dirt, but my sight's coming back slowly. I can't wear my contact lenses and that's a real problem."

"A grenade, eh? I thought you were a writer."

"I was covering a story…"

"You'll tell me all about it, I'm sure. Let's go get some of Rosita's Johnny Walker. It will rain now."

They sat around Jonas's aunt's kitchen table, sipping her scotch, and he told them the story of Salta Tigre as the afternoon rain fell fat and hard like bullets machine-gunning the roof.

"All right, but what goes on in Guatemala is no mystery," Rosita said. "Life has no value there. So, what do they want with you?"

"I don't know, but I'm starting to believe that they think I led Watson into that ambush. Maybe it's revenge, pure and simple."

"That's rather extreme, fucking Guatemalans," Hans said.

"The truth, my brother," Chevo said, "is that they don't need any reason."

"You'll stay awhile?" Rosita said.

"Two, three days, no more."

"Oh," Rosita said, "so soon."

"They'll be looking here for Vargas and me, too, and I do need to get back to Miami, see a real eye doctor. The man said I could go blind if I don't get surgery fast. But I'll be back soon this time, Rosita."

"Good. I'm so tired of these viejos."

"Have you seen Uncle Frank lately?" Hans said.

"He's good, good, living right on South Beach."

"I'd love to see him again," Hans said.

Kriegsmarine

He slept the night and most of the next day, waking late to Hans's cello, then venturing up the hills on horseback, getting used to it all again. He used to chase the horses down in the potrero behind the house, rope one, and ride bareback into the mountain howling like he imagined wild Indians would howl. Now the ride was slow and painful on his back as he followed the rows of coffee trees that terraced the colinas on their way up the mountain. He remembered Chevo telling him as a child that terracing doubled the arable land in the mountain country. The berries were red with yellow patches, almost ready to pick. The horse stopped now and then to munch on the wild grass and snort at the air, wanting to turn back. From the heights, he could see the home place and beyond, the river canyon deep as the end of the world, the Reventazón winding through the land. He noticed a Jeep raising dust far below on the crushed rock road approaching the house, and he pulled the horse around.

It was his Uncle Fritz, dark and small, ebullient and emotional, the opposite of Hans.

"Been too long, Abuelito," he said. Nobody had called him little grandfather since childhood after he got the eyeglasses with the tortoise-shell rims.

Chevo sat serious. Hans tapped his shoe. Rosita twisted her apron.

"A man is asking around for you, Jonas." Fritz said. "Stopped by El Caballo for lunch."

"Cuban," Hans said.

"He's a big, good-looking guy," Fritz said, "wears a pistol under his arm."

"¿Lo conoces?" Chevo said.

"Rosales," Jonas said.

"Rosales who?" Chevo said.

"The chief of Guatemalan presidential security."

"Válgame Dios," Rosita said.

"Fritz should bring him here," Chevo said, "and we'll find out what these cabrones want."

"Yes," Fritz said. "Then we'll control the situation."

"On one very important condition," Jonas said. "Chevo, you can't shoot him. Next they'll send the whole fucking Army after me."

"What the hell do we care?" Chevo said. "We have the fucking German Navy here to protect us."

Squeejee Island

After Jonas told him he was returning to Miami, Rosales called el Indio. "Vargas," he said, "Stay with him all the way to Miami. If we do something, it will be there, better there, anyway."

He had never seen this face on Gabriela. It was a face primordial, from the edges of the shit-covered inlet seas that brushed against the jungle, revealed when she saw what the zopilotes had left of Watson.

"I want him back here," she screamed. "He has to tell a lot."

"He's nobody, just a fucking maricón, an accident."

"How could you let him just walk out like that?"

"He was half blind and deaf from the firefight. We didn't expect it."

"He's the only one who knows what really happened, and I want to know."

"He told us what he knew. They were ambushed by guerrillas. That's all."

"I want him. I want to know every detail. I don't care what it takes. I want him back." She glared at Rosales. "Or dead."

"We set him up. It's not him. It's the war, the war."

"All right, just answer me this," she came close, her face sweating next to his. "How did he get out alive?" She bellowed like a gutted pig.

Rosales knew Gabriela felt responsible for sending Watson into the ambush and that guilt had no end, but he hated the personalization of war. He hated that she believed she had the power to kill or let live. He hated the excess. In Ramírez's case, his order was for Ramírez, not the whole family. When he cornered Vargas and stared at his impassive face, the Indian only said one word: "Gabriela." War is war. You kill the enemy, not the man, but for them it was not war, it was just Guatemala, and Jonas Harding had to die. The political conspiracy, now simplified, distilled down to Watson's death, had become a personal vendetta that, knowing Gabriela, was accelerating like a run-away locomotive toward Jonas Harding, toward an outcome that could only be satisfied by Harding's blood, no matter where, when or how.

At that moment, Gabriela's face seemed to inflate and detach itself from her neck and shoulders and bellow at him without sound. In his mind, he saw his hand pulling out the .44 and firing at the disembodied head, the bullet like all his bullets straight and true, a bullet with a heart of spent uranium, the tip encrusted with diamonds. He felt an overwhelming fatigue and thought of Laura's hands soft on his chest, before Castro, at the University of Havana where he studied English literature. He knew he would find Jonas, and at that moment he also knew he would never return to Guatemala.

Half an hour after Vargas lost him, Rosales had Jonas's destination, the flight number and had booked Vargas for the chase. One of his men at the embassy in San José followed Jonas from Juan Santamaría Airport to a house in Barrio Luján, then picked up Vargas and took him to the same house. Vargas sent him away and proceeded alone. That was the last he heard of the Indian.

The next morning, Rosales stood in front of the shack in the alley in Barrio Luján. He knocked on the door, then pushed it a little, then kicked it open. Inside he saw the little desk, one chair against the wall and one on its side on the floor. Above the chair, the wall was spattered black and he saw the bullet hole. He pushed the desk aside and dug out the bullet with his pocketknife. Probably a thirty-eight.

That was Vargas's epitaph, thirty-eight. In the back, he looked again at the fresh dirt. What do you think of your black-eyed boy now, Mr. Death? A little research at the embassy sent him to Turrialba.

El Caballo Blanco was cool and dark. A wide mirror behind the bar reflected his image and a row of tables against the wall behind him. The words Squeejee Island were painted in a red flourish in large script at the top of the mirror. He asked the bartender for an Imperial and directions to the Álvarez farm. Just tell the taxi driver to go to Las Pavas, the man said. Englishman, Rosales thought, what the hell is an Englishman doing in el culo del mundo.

U-161

Jonas rode up into the rainforest with Hans just after dawn. The horses knew the way, and Hans retold Julia's old stories, but his perspective was new to Jonas.

"Fritz and I were from the same town, Hamburg, you know."

"What's Hamburg like?"

Hans described a cold wet and dark inland seaport in the north of Germany, virtually obliterated by Allied bombings during World War II. An image from Gunter Grass told it all, he said. At dawn the eels slither up from the canal and suckle the cows. Hans said he never saw that, but to him that says everything you need to know about Hamburg.

Hans and Fritz were both from seafaring families. Hans's dad was a merchant seaman, a captain, so it made sense for Hans to join the Navy when the war broke out. He was a kid and the war was a great adventure. Everybody was for Hitler, but when England became the enemy Hans's family had problems dealing with that. Hamburg had a natural seafaring connection with the British Isles. It wasn't unusual for Hans to sail over with his father for a long weekend to buy gabardine. The English cloth was the best, his father would say, but the German tailors were better. They loved London. Hans was studying music, and it was always a treat to hear the symphony and then go pub-crawling.

He met Fritz on U-161. The submariners were heroes at the beginning of the war, and he wanted to be part of that. Fritz was a cook. Hans was on the radio. Their boat was part of a South Atlantic fleet refueled by "milk cows," underwater tankers designed to avoid combat and carry petrol to feed the regular subs. During the first years of the war, they dominated the region, sank tens of thousands of tons, but in 1943 it all turned and by 1944 the Caribbean meant suicide for U-boats. The next to final mission for U-161 brought Hans and Fritz to Costa Rican waters in July 1943. Captain Albrecht Achilles, holder of the Knight's Cross, always believed that a U-boat could somehow hit the Panama Canal. The captain's dream was for the Graf Zeppelin, a new aircraft carrier, to get close enough for one of its planes to bomb the locks, but Goering had no use for the Navy and the carrier never got out of dry dock.

There wasn't a need for much actual damage, the captain would say. If you hit a lock now and then you would close the canal permanently and tie up Allied planes, ships and personnel on both oceans. He always figured if just one of the locks or a main generator were hit, the canal would close for months, but they never made it. The Americans fortified the entire area with reconnaissance and fighter planes and brought in thousands of ground troops. That's how Hans and Fritz got here, drawn by the Canal just like Jonas's father, who enlisted to kill Nazis and ended up cooling his heels in Costa Rica during most of the war, a friend to the only two Germans he ever saw.

U-161 was worn and tired on her last run and was headed back home to refresh. But the captain wanted to hit the Canal and even though he knew that was impossible, he still didn't want to leave the Caribbean without firing a single shot at the Americans, so he asked for two volunteers. One thing, they had to speak English to pass as British sailors. That left Hans and Fritz, the only two guys from Hamburg on the boat. They realized right away that there was no coming back from the mission. They would be saboteurs and if captured would be shot. There was no POW camp for saboteurs. They would have to disappear. It was an interesting mission the captain dreamt up, very much like him, Hans said, intricate and well thought out. They couldn't sneak in anywhere near the Canal, but the main Costa Rican port of Limón, about two hundred miles above the Canal, was relatively unguarded.

"Remember, Costa Rica is not neutral," the captain had said. "Costa Rica is an enemy of the Reich." American warplanes based at La Sabana Airport in San José patrolled the coastlines all around the Canal and were supplied through Limón. Supplies traveled from Limón to San José on a narrow-gauge railroad that dated from the turn of the century and went through Turrialba on a bridge over the Reventazón River. All the supplies coming from the U.S. to San José went over that narrow bridge, so the captain decided to blow it to hell. They didn't question the mission, after all, they had survived most of the war under the captain's guidance. At the last minute, they did add one little detail. It was Fritz' idea, and they didn't tell the captain. They decided to invade Costa Rica in full uniform. They wrapped the explosive — British plastique by the way — in their Navy uniforms. They rowed ashore in a rubber dinghy at dawn and caught an early train to Turrialba. On his way back to open waters, Captain Achilles spotted the freighter San Pablo unloading at Puerto Limón and sank it with two torpedoes, killing 28 workers. The explosions stirred panic in Limón and stranded his saboteurs in Turrialba. Three months later, after refurbishing in France, U-161 sailed for the South Atlantic. It was sighted some hundred miles from Haiti by an American PBM Mariner plane and sunk with all hands.

———

Limón was United Fruit country and people were used to foreigners. Most thought the German sailors were Americans and the more observant ones thought they were British. News of the sinking of the San Pablo made it to Turrialba before they did.

They ran into Chevo at the Caballo Blanco almost as soon as they got off the train. He enjoyed using his English and they told him they were on a mission to survey the Reventazón River. Chevo told them it ran through his property and offered to take them to the bridge. Hans said they would camp there for a couple of days, and Chevo left them near the river. They looked at the bridge for two days but did nothing. It wasn't like they decided not to blow the bridge for any enlightened reason, Hans said, they just decided to survive. They started to talk about reaching San José and sitting out the war. So deciding to live, Hans said, they buried the explosives — they're still there — then tried to figure out how to get to San José.

Chevo solved their problem. He showed up with Abuelo, each of them with a Holland and Holland shotgun, and they became prisoners. What was the German Navy doing on the Reventazón? That question would remain rhetorical. But with the alarm created by the sinking of the San Pablo, they had to stay put. Later Hans liked to say, "Fishing for bobos, of course, but of course, we were the bobos."

Abuelo considered them his own private prisoners of war, and he baptized them Hans and Fritz, after a comic strip he had seen, and they were fine with that. He put them to work on the farm and before they knew it, the war was over and they never left.

"When did Dad show up?"

"Soon after we did. His plane crashed near here, you remember."

"Yes, we used to play in it."

Hans said Jonas's father had been patrolling the coastline near Limón looking for subs when he was forced to land here.

They watched the plane drop into Chevo's cornfield and plow a swath through the corn, smack into a cypress shade tree, is tail down and the nose in the air. The pilot was unconscious when they pulled him out of the cockpit, but he opened his eyes almost immediately, and Julia's face was the first thing he saw, the most beautiful thing a Jewish kid from Washington, D.C., had ever seen in his life, he liked to say.

"Didn't the Americans come to get him and the plane?"

"Yeah, they came along. Fritz and I hid in Macedonio's cave. But your dad was getting good care here. His broken leg set, he was resting nicely here at Las Pavas, and well, he wasn't too eager to leave Julia. They took the guns and the petrol out of the plane and left the rest. It's still there."

They rode toward the northern edge of the coffee fields and saw the cypress tree before they could see any part of the old plane, embraced and enveloped by the tree so that part of the trunk grew up through the length of the fuselage and out the cockpit, lifting it about five feet off the ground like the husk of a giant beetle.

Holland and Holland

Rosales felt the danger as he stepped into the cool darkness of the big house and realized that along the way he had made a crucial choice and that now it was too late to change his mind. Que maricón soy. He could have shot them all in that brief instant as he stepped into the dark foyer, but he had lost the will to do it at the foot of Vargas's grave.

"Adelante, está en su casa," Chevo said. He sat at the dining room table in the great room that adjoined the kitchen, cleaning a shotgun. Near his feet, a leather gun case held scattered metal parts and tubes of lubricant. The shotgun barrels were separated from the stock and Chevo wiped the ejectors with an oily rag. He waved the rag as Rosales extended his hand. "Sorry, I'm really greasy. Siéntese, siéntese. Fritz, how about some coffee? Homegrown, if you please."

"Cómo no," Fritz said.

"Jonas already left," Chevo said.

"I figured," Rosales said. He shifted in the chair. "We just want to clear up a couple of things…"

"Know anything about shotguns?" Chevo said.

"I know about firearms, but I've never hunted animals."

"We call animals game when we want to kill them. Well, this beauty was my dad's. Holland and Holland. Had it custom made in London. He wanted the famous Royal gun, he said, but he didn't want the gold scrollwork the lords like. He had it made smooth and clean." Chevo wiped the metal. "But he ordered something I've never seen before: he had the ejectors gold plated." Chevo lifted the barrels so Rosales could see them.

"Nice gun," Rosales said.

"Holland and Holland," Chevo said. "When I was a kid, I thought it was Holland and Holland because there were two guns, a matched pair, and each one of them was a Holland. You know — and this is truly amazing — these are Rosita's guns now. Papá didn't leave me a thing, and if we were to sell them right now, they'd be worth more than the whole goddamn farm, the house included." Chevo paused to sip his coffee. "Fritz is holding the other one, by the way, Señor Rosales, already cleaned and oiled, and it's pointed at your head."

"I know. I've been watching him in the mirror," Rosales said. He sat unmoved, calmly observing Chevo clean the shotgun. "We just need a few answers. The guerrillas killed seven of our men, including the Army chief of staff."

"I know, I know that's what you say, and I believe you, Señor Rosales, but por favor..." Chevo leaned over and gently, with respect, removed the big stainless steel .44 Smith & Wesson from Rosales's shoulder holster.

"Four-inch barrel. Good. I have a .38, but if I had a .44 I'd also go for a shorter barrel. Now I think we can talk a little better."

Rosales finished his coffee and left, escorted by Chevo and Fritz. They drove him to Turrialba and left him at the bus station. Fritz placed a glass smartly on the bar in El Caballo and poured Chevo's beer.

"What really pissed him off," Fritz said, "was that you kept the Smith & Wesson and then asked him to leave the holster, too."

"I know, I know. I'm a real jueputa." Chevo smiled with his whole face and almost started to sing a tango. "You know, Fritz, ever since Jonas came home I've acquired quite a collection, an Uzi with silencer and extra clips, two Smith & Wesson .44s, one black, and three really fine German cuchillas. Not bad for a farmer without land living in a shanty, wouldn't you say?"

Macedonio's cave

The horses knowing the way lumbered on their own up the hills, their hooves patting at the red clay. Jonas could have been riding up on this very trail thirty years earlier following Abuelo's bay around the terraced mountain, the old man telling his angry stories. The old man would always get angry when he told the stories.

In his favorite story, a young man about thirty or so walked slowly in the dark. He's nearsighted and night blind and only a quick lunar flicker now and then keeps him on the dirt road. On one side of the road, a sheer drop falls into a ferment of black-green, an abyss of treetops. The sounds of the forest are the warm moist wind and the billion insects, a thousand for every star, the sound in waves, like the sea. Then he hears horses. Three men come up to him and talk until the usual greetings turn silent and then two of them shove him, again and again. The eyeglasses with the thin round tortoise-shell rims snap to the gravel. The third man smashes his chest with an axe handle.

Jonas could almost hear his grandfather's voice telling the story. The night was black, the old man says, and he was not hurt. He was strong and the bruising beating seemed to glance off his jacket. But he knows they will kill him, blind, now, without his glasses. He can feel wet blood, cool on his skin in the night air. Sereno means dusk in Spanish, and it also means cool dusk breeze, and it means he is the one who is vigilant in the night, and it means calm, too, and that is why once many years later the old man said that should be his name, but it didn't stick. Then Rojas, ahh, there was the betrayal. Then Rojas, who had been Abuelo's manager, Rojas who organized the coffee harvest, puts the gun to Abuelo's head and squeezed the trigger.

When he tells the story, the old man relives his anger and tells it with anger. His blind eyes see a light, but it isn't the flash of the gun. It's before the gunshot and it causes his head to adjust toward the brightness, just so, ever so slightly, the angle of the shot shifting imperceptibly, the bullet whisking his skull, over his right ear.

It's very dark. The men roll him to the drop-off. They know the wilderness will consume him. Even here, hidden from the vultures, the tiny faithful will perform their duty coming down from the green canopies and up from the terraced labyrinths of the red earth. There would be nothing left. Even the bones would be scattered by the congregation.

The night here is different. The northern night has a cold, clear darkness. But the night of the jungle is thick, layered, textured, resistant to penetration and yet, at a particular point, yielding and enveloping as it receives a familiar body — *my land recognizes me* — and the night gently accepts it, rolling it into Macedonio's cave. The man awakens to water dripping and sunlight shining rainbows on the ceiling of the cave, restoring his sight. A rock shelf hidden by foliage not more than five feet from the edge of the dirt road had stopped his fall, rolling him in and then dropping him another few feet into the cave. Perhaps once an Indian tomb, now it was Macedonio's secret workshop. The quartz ceiling glitters with gathering moisture that condenses and drips into a pool near his head. All around stand Macedonio's silent wood sculptures, the brown mahogany faces of their Spanish and Indian ancestors gazing soberly at him.

And that's how he didn't die and had seven children, and that's how Jonas had the opportunity to wail into life thirty years later, pushed from the belly of Abuelo's second daughter.

Hans hummed the Kol Nidrei as they rode slowly up the hills. Jonas knew very little about Judaism, but this song was part of his life, and as they approached the summit of the terraced hills, he thought how appropriate to leave all the old promises to other gods behind in a combined confession and absolution and as he thought about that, about abandoning all vows, he realized that he could hear clearly now, the horses breathing and their hooves on the red clay.

Hans pointed to the ledge that hid the entrance to Macedonio's cave. "If you look about five feet up from the ledge, you'll see it." They dismounted and climbed the steep crevice. The temperature dropped instantly as they entered the cave's sudden darkness. He could hear the water dripping as he followed Hans around a bend into a festival of flashing quartz crystal rainbows.

CHAPTER SEVEN

Havana Hallelujah

Oye, timbero yo la quiero
Ay, con mucho desespero
vamos a ver,
Habana, ella es toda mi ilusión
— LETRAS RUMBA GUAGUANCÓ YAMBÚ,
COLUMBIA ABAKUÁ LYRICS

The calling

No land in sight as night fell, and the little outboard was still in the deep water of the Florida Straits, the wind picking up. The compass needle points north, he thought, and you follow the bottom of the needle south all the way to Havana. That's all there is to it. Cuba is south and the needle points north. Ah, but then he remembered, there's a drift. You must adjust for the Gulf Stream drift. It's pulling north. But how can it pull north when the pull is to your left, and you're heading at a right angle to the pull? And then there's the bigger drift, the rotation of the earth, but the stars are fixed, and they can tell you where you are... floating in the Straits in the bile black sea puttering somewhere. Then there's the wind picking up

117

and the waves and speed in knots, knots.

I shouldn't talk of bile, he thought too late, retching into the wind. Not into the wind, asshole, but then there's wind all around. He looked for the stars but his salt-spattered glasses blinded him. He cleaned them on the windbreaker, and then the surf slapped his face again hard, ripping the glasses away.

God help me understand, if I want to head southeast, why do I point west? A la mano de Dios, he thought, and caught himself from finishing the one-line prayer with y María Santísima as he rolled hard against the sides of the little outboard. One star, sweet Jesus, one star I can understand is all I need to fulfill your vision. Black hair and beard dripping, he tied down the rudder and used the rest of the rope to lash himself to the middle seat. He pulled the blue tarp over his head and fell exhausted into the well between the benches, pulling his knees close to his great stomach and sobbed, not because he was afraid of death, he had prepared for that, but because for the first time in his forty-eight years, the Reverend Mario Núñez truly felt the presence of God — in the little boat, out there all around, high above and deep below, and he, Núñez, bobbing imperceptibly in the immensity of the cold sea, inside the blur of the darkening heavens, a tiny speck inside His universe.

"¿Dónde tu vas, maricón?"

A sudden thud and violent rocking awakened him. Blinking up first at a blinding sun and then at the dark silhouette of a man standing over him, Núñez turned to see the massive gray hull of a Cuban gunboat, looming huge next to his rocking outboard, and then he twisted around, lifting himself, his hair dripping, gasping for breath, he saw the sunlit bay and beyond, the ramparts of Old Havana.

El Manicomio

Her eyes closed, her face disfigured by strain and sweat, María curled an over-weighted barbell. She opened her eyes to a spartan gray gym, a few beefy men lumbering around stacks of loose weights and focused on the face of a man standing before her holding a towel. Jorge Barrientos, the Mental Ward's second in command, looked at her stiffly.

"Hola, Jorge," she said straining against the weight of the barbell as she nestled it back on the rack.

"Hola Sor María, welcome back." He lobbed the towel at her. She snatched it out of the air and wiped her face. "Águila wants us up in interrogation." He never smiled.

Águila sat in the shadows. Behind him, an immense poster of an angry Uncle Sam pointed a gnarled finger over his head at María. Don't call me Águila, he would say, regretting the youthful bravado that had provoked the nickname he had earned en la Sierra, but it stuck to him as he rolled into Havana in the first wave on January 3, 1959, with Eloy Gutiérrez Menoyo, bearded and boastful, oozing with the sweaty exhausttion of an ecstasy like fucking. It was an official nom-de-guerre, they would say, and he couldn't shrug it off. She always figured that had more to do with his profile than anything else, for the boss had a prodigious aquiline nose that in combination with his stooped posture and bald oval-shaped head gave him an aggressive avian aspect. Only nicknames or first names were allowed in the Mental Ward in case of bugs, and the boss liked to be called Carlos instead of Águila. But sometimes María called him Águila just to mess with him a little, and when he would look at her frowning she would laugh, "We got to keep the fascists confused, right chico?" Then his face would soften. She had loved him with a daughter's tenderness ever since he found her a few days after the triumph of the revolution in a pauper's clinic in Vedado, delusional and starving, with a few other freed political prisoners. He wrapped her in a blanket and carried her to a hospital. "You were in a police station jail near the clinic where two men dropped you off," he told her years later. "You were half-dead. One was a Batista cop and the other one was Manolo Rosales. He lived nearby and was known at the clinic."

Carlos had connected Rosales, a known CIA spook in Venezuela, to the 1976 Cubana de Aviación DC-8 bombing, and Rosales became an essential and missing part of her memory. She had been tortured in jail and somehow awak-ened, perhaps days later in the clinic. Unable to walk or move her left arm, she lay there in and out of consciousness until Águila found her. She had one solid image of her torture — a number tattooed on the guard's chest and was certain that Rosales owned that tattoo and the answers she needed. She found his step-mother's house near the clinic, now subdivided by the revolution and was assigned two rooms on the top floor. She looked for him, but he never came back. She traced him from Caracas to Guatemala, but Salta Tigre swept that away. Now, perhaps, he could become the mission.

Carlos looked the same now, one of those men who appeared older at thirty and then never aged. While she recovered, she worked in his office as a clerk. That was right after the victory, during the time of political cleansing and most of the work was in Havana. Later when she was fully recov-ered, he sent her to Moscow for training and slowly integrated her into intelligence work throughout the Americas. Águila won his merit in the Sierra and was later rewarded with government responsibility. He learned spycraft in Moscow and then came home to organize the Mental Ward in a large corner townhouse on Avenida de Las Américas.

"Hola, Carlos," she said, managing a smile.

"You look thin... and tired," he said in English. His conversations with her were always in English, to avoid the curious, he said.

"You too," she said.

"Got a little sidetracked in Salta Tigre, did you..."

"It was just a recon. There was no activity there. I was on my way to Guatemala City."

"I know... Rosales."

"I had the O.K. on that."

"Claro, and you still do."

"Who could know that colonel in the jungle was the chairman of the joint chiefs of the whole fucking Guatemalan Army. I wasn't ready to leave Guatemala."

"And your priest was a Miami reporter. He made it back O.K., but he hasn't written a word about Salta Tigre or anything else."

"Others have. Now they say this proves the insurgency wiped out Salta Tigre."

"We're working on that, but the important thing is that even though we didn't plan it that way, villagers all the way to Honduras know that Salta Tigre was avenged. That they are not alone, helpless. I know you need a break, but you'll have to take it in Miami.

"Miami?"

Facing him, in a harsh half-light, she smoked a cigarette, glancing restlessly up at the ceiling, down at the cigarette as he talked, then squarely at his face and at Uncle Sam. He did look thinner, she thought, and too carefully dressed in a long-sleeved guayabera usually reserved for special events. She noticed his hands, calmly turning the pages in a folder — the nails carefully filed, not the sun-darkened hands she remembered, the guajiro cane-cutter and guarapo juicer-hands. She shivered a little. Had the guerrilla changed, had Águila totally morphed into Carlos? Then he handed her the file on the Reverend Mario Núñez. As she read, Carlos scratched the back of his head, as if Uncle Sam were breathing down his collar.

She suppressed a laugh. "Is he for real? Boats don't float into Havana in the night, they float away from Havana…"

"That's not funny," Barrientos said. She had forgotten he was in the room. Barrientos, the Manicomio's political officer had tried to ingratiate himself with the staff but failed. He had no field experience and worst of all did not have Águila's revolutionary heritage. He wrote periodic reports on the Manicomio's activities for the higher ups. The reports carried Águila's signature, but on occasion Águila received an inquiry, which he knew had not been officially reported, usually related to María's field work. "No confíes en él," don't trust him, Águila told her. "He's a little twisted."

Águila conceded that the preacher could be CIA. "But there's no trace of that, and we've checked. He has a church in Hialeah, but he's really a nobody in Miami," Águila said. "The man's on a mission for Jesus Christ, and he has a plan."

"For Jesus Christ," María said, "and he has a plan. A nobody from Miami has a plan."

"Tranquila, tranquila. Take it easy. It made us think… something, that if handled correctly could put a crack in the American embargo, especially now with Jimmy Carter."

"Carter won't last, and everything could change next year with a new American president."

"Just turn around. Vira p'atras," he said, pointing his chin at the mirror behind her as it becomes transparent, revealing Núñez, an obese figure natty in a khaki prison jump suit, gesticulating, stabbing the air with a large cigar in silent animated conversation with someone out of view. Suddenly, Núñez's adenoidal voice envelops them in the soundproof room, oddly sonorous, as if broadcast from another country. He's not católico, apóstlico ni romano, Núñez says. He sees himself as Evangelical by nature and any measure, but not nearly Pentecostal. His mission, however, is not to preach, he says, but to lead the faithful into a promised land of hope and restoration.

"Lead them where, chico?" a modulated voice outside of the window frame asked in a friendly, chummy tone. Núñez rises, pounds his fist on the table and appears to look around triumphantly as he pumps the cigar.

"Havana, chico."

Núñez sits down and brushes his hand over his head. The one-way mirror goes black and María turns from the shadow back into the harsh half-light, facing Carlos.

"What the fuck does he want?"

"He wants to bring little old Cuban exile ladies from Miami, from New Jersey, wherever, to visit their relatives in Cuba."

"Bring little old gusanos back?"

Carlos leaned forward, a new lively look in his eye.

"Not gusanos, chica, la comunidad, the blessed community."

That's the old Águila at work again, thinking again, she thought. The concept was pure, geometric in its clarity, the kind of political and economic leverage that would make

Archimedes proud. She understood the Greeks. She would be a doctor after all.

"The strongest political force working against us is the undying relentless hatred of the Cuban exiles in the United States." He paused, not wanting to rush, thinking it out and savoring the thinking. "And, paradoxically, the strongest desire of the Cuban exiles in the United States is to reach out to their families in Cuba... in a way that is legal, that is sanctioned..."

"Give them what they desire, not what they demand," Barrientos said.

"So, what do we get out of it?" she said.

"Dollars. Millions. Maybe ten million per month. Foreign exchange and international goodwill up the wazoo," Águila said.

"But, will the gringos go for it?"

"We think so. At first, anyway, they'll give the gusanos what they want. Then later they'll feel a pinch of regret and react one way or another. But we're working on the political angle here and in Washington, and there's a special mission in Panama right now talking with some prominent Miamians interested in rapprochement putting together a rationale for this — the core of the project could be an exchange of political prisoners."

"Exchange them for what?"

"Goodwill dollars. Miami is your job."

"How do I start?"

"First, you make sure those maniacs in Miami don't waste Núñez. Second, you go into the travel agency business. The cover company — Havana Tours — is already set up in Kingston." He hands her a key. "The usual system — cash, equipment and instructions at the Flagship Bank in Coral Gables. There will be much more cash than usual in the box.

Open a checking account for Havana Tours right there and deposit the bulk of the cash. Our only contact will be through the box, or in Kingston. Phone calls only from Kingston. Coded telexes through Santo Domingo."

María stepped out of the half-light and into the shadow, approaching the door.

"And there's a bonus," he said as she reached the door and stopped, not turning. "Rosales is back in Miami."

María stepped back.

"But he's not the primary mission," Barrientos said. "Don't forget that."

"We're towing the Reverend back to Key West in five days," Águila said. She turned for a second and focused on his hands, jaundiced in the half-light and heard him say, "Oh, and, María, good work, chica." He couldn't see her smile.

Say Kaddish for me

María can't see the face of the man leaning over her as he reaches, pinning her shoulders to the table. Another man grasps her ankles. She is a woman who has not been touched that much, and no man has ever held her ankles, and for the briefest moment the hands on her ankles feel like a caress, tightening. They whip her breasts and stomach with truncheons. She screams and whimpers like a goat before the kill but says nothing. Then they hit her head and shoulders and her left clavicle snaps. She screams again. Cuidado, cabrón, don't you know shit, the other one says, push the pain just enough, just enough. If you go too far, they pass out. If you go too far, they give up and die. They flip her on her stomach and jab the truncheon into her vagina, then deeply into her rectum. They start to cut her leg, little cuts first then into the bone. She

screams the names and places they want to hear. Ahora sí.
Now you can do anything you want. Darkness envelops her,
but jostling awake, she feels herself lifted and hears two men.
She'll never forget their voices, but the words slip in and slip
out. "Manolo, aguántala tú, las piernas, que tiene la clavícula
rota. Grab her legs, I can see the clavicle ripping through her
skin. The clinic is right there. Mother of God, who did this?
Through the unbuttoned khaki shirt of the man above her, she
focuses on the markings of a number tattooed on his chest.
The purple trembling number looks like 4711. Eau de
Cologne, she thinks, and then nothing.

Sitting on the cement front steps of her large townhouse on Calle 14 just off the Avenida de Las Américas, Esther darned her sons' socks. Plucking the socks from two baskets next to her, the darned and the undarned, she slipped a large white glass egg into a sock and mended assiduously with aggressive sure twists of her wrist. The big house was subdivided into apartments, and Esther lived comfortably downstairs with a little kitchen, a parlor and her bedroom. María had two rooms on the attic level.

"Hola, chica," she said.

"T'esperaba," Esther said. "Dame otra," she said, pointing her chin at the undarned. And so, their relationship began, mending holes in socks that would never be worn by sons who would never come home. María's work was solitary, but it did allow for some luxuries, and she would take Esther to the diplomatic stores for canned asparagus and Polish ham.

With Carlos's help, María had worked out the identities of the two men who left her in the clinic on the eve of the revolution's triumph. They were Esther's stepsons, and they lived near the clinic. Pulling some strings, she managed to rent two rooms in Esther's house and over time, the two women warmed to each other.

"Why didn't you go to Miami?" María asked one day. Esther was thoughtful. The boys were grown, with their own lives, so she would have been alone anyway. "No, not me. Estoy en casa. And besides, she said, bringing her face close to María's, laughing at the irony, "Soy roja!"

On Sundays, they would walk along the Malecón in the afternoon and stop at Copelia for ice cream along the way, two ordinary women, the eternal sea breeze cooling their faces, licking ice cream cones.

After a long absence during her training in Moscow, María returned with gifts and stories of the Russians and of a side trip to Kaunas, and Esther asked, why did you go to Kaunas, of all places? Just because of you, María said. I wanted to see the place you came from. Now I can see you here and understand more about you and your family.

———

In civilian clothes, María is an attractive professional woman in her thirties just leaving work as she steps out of the building on Avenida de las Américas into the super bright Havana afternoon, throws her bag into an open, dilapidated red VW Beetle convertible and races through Spanish colonial Havana, honking, downshifting into turns and gunning the car onto the country highway. She floors it for about 30 minutes until she slows into the old Jewish cemetery in Guanabacoa.

The cemetery, slightly overgrown but not unkempt, glistens white, ample and quiet. "Nice car. Are you family?" The caretaker, a tall guajiro, face red and sweaty under yellow hair, offers a calloused hand.

"No. Just a friend. Vivíamos cerca. The family's in Miami."

He pulls an empty coffin, a light gray box with holes on the bottom, easily from an ancient Chevy station wagon and stands it on end against the wall of a compact, whitewashed structure near the cemetery gate. The entrance is doorless, and she can see Esther's corpse on a counter near the doorway covered by a white sheet, the soles of her feet shining.

Three women, also in white, work over her. One at the head, the other in the middle and the third one at the feet, they lift the body and place it, still covered, into a large trough. They submerge the body and lift it three times. Placing it then again on the counter, they cover it with a white shroud and pat it dry, working under the cloth. María spots Yitzhak Belman ambling up the gravel roadway. An old acquaintance of Esther, Belman, 80, would sometimes join them on their walks along he Malecón. He loves the ice-cream cones from Copelia.

The guajiro slides the coffin to the front of the doorway and the women accommodate Esther into it. María and Belman follow the four of them as they struggle to carry it, the sides of the box buckling like cardboard, to the edge of the cemetery overlooking a valley spiked with palm trees and lower it into the waiting open ground.

A slight, stooped man in a Panama hat waits until they finish.

"I didn't know there were any rabbis left in Cuba," María said.

"I'm not a rabbi. I just know the El Malei — you remember it?"

"I'm not Jewish."

The man wipes his face, aims a nod of recognition at Belman looking around at the cemetery as if expecting others, wanting others, then chants to himself quietly. She heard a word of Hebrew now and then.

"Esther Schuster..." he said.

"Esther Schuster..." The speaker finishes, glances quickly at María and hurries off. Belman walks up to the open grave. "¿Dónde la pongo?" Where do I put it? He vacillates for a moment, then lays a small rock next to the grave. María kneels on one knee and lets a handful of pebbles filter down through her fingers, whispering on the coffin lid.

Delirium in a dream

Hey, it's me, I tell myself, I'm Jonas Harding, and I'm back in Uncle Frank's Miami Beach apartment. I know I'm me, still hurting and half blind, but a force in this dream has total control and drags me along. Somehow my eyes are all healed up. I can see forever. I'm in my old British-racing-green Triumph Spitfire, the one I totaled years ago on U.S. 29 near Gaines Run heading to Charlottesville, Virginia, top down, booming north on I-95 the way only a Triumph can boom, a deep echoing growl. It's a clear morning with a blue sky, feathery angel clouds gathering. No radio, no music, nothing to interfere with the roar of the Spitfire as we whiz past Boca on the way to Palm Beach. Wind down to third. Exit. There's a Rolls parked in the circular driveway at the Breakers, a monster hotel from another century. It's not a car, it's the Jazz Age itself polished, deep gray-blue and brown. The ticket says Lot No. 101, Phantom II, Sedanca Coupe, 1932.

I unleash the Leicas and get a low frontal shot with the 28mm, looking up at the Victorian towers, enlarging the front left fender into the foreground. The audience has already found seats for the auction, and I hear the hammer hit the block. I had wanted to shoot the items on display first, but I'll get them later. Usually the stuff stays around a while. The new features editor had a wart big as quarter on her chin. I had never seen her before. She told me to be sure to shoot the little black dress. And shoes, I said, kidding, no she said, she was barefoot in that dress, but get the hat. The editor got a kick sending me to shoot an auction. I had just returned from Central America and still stank of dirt and decay, but to her I'm an ingénu. "You can't write. Might as well shoot." At least I'd get to run the Spitfire.

I found an empty aisle seat in the third row and looked around for Rolls bidders. I plopped the camera bag down, perhaps a little too heavily, and a woman next to me turned to look. Her legs must have been crossed because one bare foot brushed the bag and lingered there for a moment. She was wearing a black silk hat tight around her head with only a few strands of blond hair showing and a light coat with a fur collar.

"It's a refrigerator in here," I said, fingering one of the Leicas in my bag.

She turned gazing at me through a thin black veil adorned with little, tiny black flowers that came down to her lips. The door in back opened again and the sunlight spotlighted her face, diffusing her features as it highlighted her gray eyes. She leaned over slightly, her legs still crossed, and flipped open the top of the camera bag with her foot. Inside, three Leicas sat nestled like Faberge eggs. Her toes touched all three, moving them only slightly, as if to ascertain model of body and focal length of lens. This is not real, I tell myself, but let it carry me on.

"Bet you're bidding on the Phantom," I said, grabbing one of the Leicas and quickly snapping a couple of shots of her and the room.

She turned, facing me completely, lifted the veil and brought her mouth to mine, kissing it tenderly, her hand on my neck. The smell was musk, but with a jagged edge of Chanel. She gave me little kisses, pulling back now and then to look at me, and returning. The tip of her tongue outlined my lips and then slowly found its way into my mouth. In one quick determined motion, she raised the coat and was on my lap, facing me, one of my hands crazy on small breasts and hard nipples, the other pressing on the hollow at the small of her back and we were joined in a slow ebb-and-flow tide of delicious unvulcanized fucking.

The hammer hit the block again, and the door opened like a shutter on the spotlight, blinding me as I tried to catch my breath thinking desperately how the hell am I going to get out of this, and as I zipped my pants I saw the chair next to me empty and my camera bag gone.

I was out of there like redlining the Spitfire in first and in the lobby I saw immediately that it would be impossible to find her. Hundreds of persons milled around the displays as the auctioneer's cadence rolled along. Old ladies from Palm Beach fingered the treasures, carefully extricating baroque silver amulets from leather pouches. On one table, a series of documents, photos and other scrapbook memories framed a symmetrical display built around a Life magazine cover, in black and white, with her sitting in a chair, the black dress one with the dark background so she appeared as all long white legs, bare toes, arms and face, her chin resting on both hands, elbows on the crossed knees, a bemused expression in her light gray eyes. The edges were torn and an abrasion left a smudge where the type should have been. I looked up at the soaring ceilings, Jesus. I still felt a sensual satisfied weakness, now enhanced by a vaulting sense of absolute dis-orientation.

"Mr. Harding –"

I never met a real butler, but this guy was what you'd imagine a real butler would look like — an older man, thinning dark hair slicked down neatly, a thin moustache decorating a self-satisfied grin. He leaned forward slightly from the waist of his tuxedo, toward me, my camera bag in his gray-gloved hand.

"I believe this belongs to you."

The three black Leicas were still there, but the lenses had been removed and placed aside, the baseplates beside them as if someone had taken the film and failed to close the cameras. The black paint on the cameras was worn off, and the yellow brass glinted at me. The ladies from Palm Beach chirped along. The Spitfire was still there. I roared onto I-95 south, letting the hot air and the diesel fumes purify my soul. The sun was higher, hot now, and it was glorious on my face, blinding, like the festival of flashing quartz rainbows from Macedonio's cave.

Laura's Café

Awakening in a white haze, I rubbed the white gauze from my left eye and rolled off the couch, stumbling into the kitchen of Uncle Frank's one-bedroom apartment. The coffee was still warm.

I walked out of the old Art Deco hotel converted into one bedroom and efficiency condos onto the hot Miami Beach blacktop street one block behind the ocean and hailed a cab.

"Calle Ocho y la 37."

Able to see only shadows and bright patches out of one eye and mostly a blur out of the other, and unable to drive from my home in Kendall, I knew I would have to move closer in, but for now Uncle Frank's apartment was a haven.

Some two dozen chanting demonstrators wave placards in front of the newspaper's Little Havana neighborhood office. Two men appear to be chained to the doors of the nondescript building, nestled in the Plaza Miramar strip mall between a cigar store with a small espresso coffee window and the Chévere gay bar, sort of hidden away in the crook of the L. As the cab pulls up in front of Laura's Café on Calle Ocho, across the street from my new office, I decide to go for coffee and avoid the mob.

Laura, a tall, handsome woman in her forties with obviously tinted long black hair, dressed in a black pantsuit and a low-cut blouse that reveals the tops of her breasts swelling out of the tender lace of a flamingo-colored bra, places a small cup of Cuban espresso and a folded newspaper on the table. Her face is heavily made up in blacks and reds. Now I know she's Rosales's ex-wife.

Her little boy comes up with a box of dominoes and without a word sets them up.

"What's the problem over there." I nod toward the newspaper office.

"The fucking paper did it again," she said.

"What's the bitch?"

"Front page story about a baseball bat factory in Havana."

"Yea, they're trying to get closer to the community."

"The one here, or the one there? And you never mention the political prisoners in Cuban jails, the torture and the abuse of the prisoners. And now this."

She slams the newspaper on the table spilling dominoes and coffee on the Living section. Laura's Café is on column one of the food page.

"You say my food stinks, that the ropa vieja is horrible, the tostones are soggy and my son shouldn't be bothering the customers."

'Hold it. It's not me, Laura. I don't even cover Miami. Lemme see that." I grabbed the paper and left the table. In the hallway on the way out, I see a large display of photographs under a Cuban flag and a banner that reads "La Brigada."

I put a finger on the photo of Manolo Rosales standing arm in arm with a group of seven thin and scruffy young men in swim trunks in front of a swimming pool. One of the men is black. Laura comes up and places a hand on my shoulder.

"Look, I'm sorry about that."

"Forget about it. I understand."

"My ex. Cute isn't he? Can't stand to live with him, but I still love him."

"I met him once, in Guatemala. He was at Playa Girón?"

"Yes. He was with the first group of prisoners released after the Bay of Pigs. Castro traded them all for five hundred tractors. That picture is at the Dupont Plaza hotel."

"How many prisoners came back?"

"About fifteen hundred, all CIA trained and defeated, looking for revenge. We were crazy in love and I was there to welcome him home, but we couldn't stay at the Dupont that night. One of the ex-prisoners was black and when he arrived later that day, they wouldn't let him register at the Dupont. So all seven moved to another hotel."

"Hell of a welcome home."

"Yes. That's the way it was back then."

I grabbed a cab and headed downtown to the main office building on the bay. The demonstration had arrived before me and the chants — "Free the political prisoners" — echoed off the massive building. The first time I saw that crystal palace, it took my breath away. The entire building of my newspaper in Virginia could fit in the foyer.

Two demonstrators had chained themselves to the main doors of the building. "Fuck you, cocksucker," one of them said as I pushed past them.

The newsroom

Rosy had already told me I should report to the Little Havana office, so I didn't have a desk, and I had to pick up my stuff. The paper had gone electronic while I was away, and now big green screens cast a ghastly color everywhere. I looked for the Living Today desk and parked myself in front of one of the monitors.

The activity of the newsroom closed around me like an enveloping green velvet curtain, choking my breath, brushing my face as I tried to contain it, until I disappeared.

The desktop was impersonal, yellowish green metal with a rubbery surface under my fingertips. On top of it, roundly distorted by the computer screen, my reflected face blinked sea-green alphabets. I stared at the eye-patched pirate's face faintly fluttering back from the screen, blinking green nausea and fear at me. I'm looking more, with time, like my grandfather, I thought. Thinking of the old man filled me with warmth, and at that moment I wanted to go back to Turrialba. That was new.

Swiveling the chair, I took in the long full panorama of the newsroom at work on the early afternoon "bulldog" edition, as Rosy liked to call it. He liked to sneer "bulldog" in the afternoon news meeting, to unnerve the copy desk. I knew now, after Salta Tigre, that I could never satisfy the newspaper, could no longer muster any interest in the details of building stories, and the newspaper was angry, demanding sacrifice. I was afraid to fully admit it to myself because I didn't know what else to do with my life.

When I regained most of my sight after surfacing from the pit at Salta Tigre, there was a rush of elation, a feeling of immortality, and later I continued to think of Salta Tigre as somewhat liberating, tucked in an unknown place, in a time frame all its own. But I couldn't shake a lingering core of guilt and fear kindled by that experience that emanated from my guts orbiting around in a moon-cycle, an inexorable black tide pulling at me rhythmically.

Persons in business attire conversed in modulated voices above the quiet tapping of computer keyboards. No one looks at anyone, I thought.

Next to me in the sterile sprawling modern office, large as an indoor stadium dominated by the robotic CRT screens, two women in pastel cotton suits rap their hard fingernails on the emerald glass. My face is just level with their butts.

"Bring that graph up. That's your lead," the butt closest to me said.

"No way, I like it as a kicker."

"You reviewed Laura's Café in today's paper?" I said to near-butt.

"Yes," near-butt answered without turning.

"The question is why? Why the hell pan a little breakfast joint in Little Havana."

"We're trying to get closer to the community, haven't you heard?"

"Well the community doesn't like it."

I suddenly felt weak and realized I hadn't really recovered yet. With excruciating effort, I pushed myself back from the desk, perhaps too brusquely, hitting near-butt hard, shoving her into the other woman, a senseless, pathetic act emanating from a distant lost place.

The buttock owner whirled as though she had been waiting a lifetime for that opportunity. The face she glimpsed was alien, dark, darkened by sun and by blood — my grandfather and then even his father — high cheekbones and thin, black moustache. Had her slight, almost translucent, eggshell hand smacked my face smartly, cleanly, perhaps the ass bumping would have been only another reprimand, another item in the folder, but the diamond on her hand whisked my right eye eyebrow (I saw it as a flashing pinprick) slicing into the stitches. There was too much blood to leave it at that.

Rosy Rosenfeld shrugged his shoulders, as I passed by his glass-enclosed office into the executive editor's larger rooms overlooking Biscayne Bay. I thought of Rosy's last lecture, the wash-my-hands lecture he gave before sending me to Little Havana. "Lookit," Rosy's stare locked on me, quiet, serious, leaning closer, his baldness glinting, just put one word in front of the other. It's like walking — one foot in front of the other. Very few reporters get that opportunity. You were there for Chrissake. Then, liven it up. Put some fucking adjectives in. Do an adjective sweep after you finish the story. Put one in before each fucking noun. You remember what a fucking adjective is don't you, Jonas?"

"Yea, it's just one foot in front of another."

"Wind it up with some fucking metaphors. Then some conceptual shit. Throw in some opinion…"

"Opinion," I said.

"It's a first-person story, of course, you asshole."

I could see Rosy thinking perhaps of his own father, a Republican judge in Milwaukee, and then staring out the window at the fucking bay, rubbing his nose with his knuckles like a prizefighter. Then, quietly, "just write something, anything. We'll clean it up."

Rosy was hurt, now. He looked at me like "you don't know how hard it is for me to tell you these things, these obvious things, you shithead, and I don't ever want to hear myself saying them again so I won't tell you...."

I wanted then to scream back but couldn't. I wanted to scream back — I can't believe you are telling me to do a fucking adjective sweep, you piece of shit. Rosy looked very tired and he looked at me with pity, almost nausea, as I sat there in front of the bay, refusing to write.

Now, weeks after that scene, with one eye freshly patched and no perspective, I looked at Rosy, past the conference table through Tom Bruton's glass-walled office, and past him at the sky over the bay and then again at Rosy turning and at his rounded shoulders in the white wet-armpit dress-shirt.

"You're suspended," Bruton said, "You can't pull this shit in my newsroom. Who the hell do you think you are? Being a good reporter isn't enough. It wasn't enough to make up for not writing in the best news town in America, and it's not enough to make up for this kind of bullshit."

As I watched Bruton be angry in his cold, corporate way, I imagined the starched brain thinking stiffly, synapses crackling at the edges. Bruton swiveled his chair, breathing deeply, giving me his back and answered his secretary through the glass on the intercom. Mabel's modulated voice, routinely, knowingly, told Bruton of things only he understood as she stared through the glass at the sun-tanned man, blood dripping from his bandaged eye.

Outside the executive editor's glass cage, the quiet insistent tapping of computer keys continued in the newsroom but slowed as several reporters stopped to watch and a group formed quietly in front of the window that exposed Bruton's office to the newsroom. I rubbed my face, pressing on the sharp insistent cut, only encouraging the blood to seep through the bandage, sprinkling my white shirt, making an impression on the nondescript tie. Bruton talked on, waving his arms, and then turning slowly, focused for an instant on his window's privileged horizon, glittering past the bay, and then his gaze lowered, settling on me sitting impassive, bleeding.

"Mother of god, he's hemorrhaging, Mabel. Mabel, get me a goddamn towel. Mabel, a towel, for Chrissake." At that moment, something strangely charitable enveloped Bruton's attitude, the look in his eye. I could see sunlight glint off the blond hairs on his long rabbit face, a thoughtful face, looking about for confirmation, as if clinging to belief in a primordial stone that remained uncaring, oblivious.

"Jonas, what the hell is going on? This is not like you. No, no, no, not like you, ever."

He believed in me, he said. His pink face, now redder expressing anguish, appeared to crave belief in the absence of any rational confirmation from me that belief was justified, belief despite the absolute confirmation that he had been betrayed by his own need to believe in his reporter. Bruton looked down at his thick wrists and long fingers probably thinking of his tennis serve — he'd missed the first one, now hit the second ball deftly, in the corner, just brushing the line.

Bruton handed me the towel. I raised it to my eyes and placed it there, leaning back, letting it gently cover my face.

"I know you'll write that story," he said, almost to himself, still looking down. "For now, you're on suspension for two weeks. You'll lose the pay of course, and then probation for— I don't know — a goddamn year. When you get back, we'll meet with Rosy. This is the best news town in America."

"I know it," I said, peeling the towel off, placing it on Bruton's desk.

Bruton pointed to the door of his private washroom. "Wash up in there."

I sat down on the commode watching him through the just open door of the lavatory. Bruton pulled the cord on the blinds, shutting out the newsroom and plucked the wet towel from the desktop, holding it in both hands, gazing at the bloody imprint. "Jesus Christ," he said, "the goddamn shroud of Turin."

"He needs therapy," Bruton said as Rosy appeared in my field of view.

"He needs a kick in the ass, right out of here," Rosy said.

"You always thought he was good."

"I hired him, didn't I? But that experience in Guatemala fucked him up, and there's nobody we can talk to, but..."

"No, and we can't fire him now, not that I really want to anyway. He's become a sort of celebrity for the moment. The irony is that the Pulitzer is a sure thing if he ever writes the goddamn story. Let's revisit when he gets back. Keep him in Little Havana for now on the new Spanish edition. Maybe editing on the copy desk. That'll help us a lot and would get him out of this newsroom for a while," Bruton said.

"Yes, he does know the language, but he's not Cuban. He's a half-Jewish Costa Rican half-gringo."

"Jesus Christ, let's not get into that. We're already on press with the Spanish edition and you know we can't find enough bilingual editors. Anything else happening in the world today?"

"The demonstrators are still out there," Rosy said.

"I know. Make sure nobody does anything, says anything. Leave them alone. They'll get tired. And make sure we have a story in the bulldog."

"The baseball bat story really pissed them off."

I know, but we can't bend our coverage to the anti-Castro crazies."

"It's more than that though. The new Spanish edition really has them upset."

"You'd think otherwise. Its only got a five-year life span at most. Spanish readers are dwindling," Bruton said.

"Then they'll blame us for killing the thing."

"Of course. Also, I hear a pretty high U.S. official, somebody close to President Carter, was in Cuba last weekend," Bruton said.

"Do we have a story?"

"No. It was my own source — super confidential. We can't use it."

"Carter looking for rapprochement — I'll find a way to nail that down." Rosy faded away as I left. Bruton, his back to me, didn't notice.

Standing a few feet away from the building's entrance under the soaring awning, holding a Bacardi rum cardboard box filled with files and notebooks, I noticed a street sign that proclaimed, "Dead End." The demonstrators were gone, but one man still chained to a door slept peacefully next to a placard that read: "FREE THE POLITICAL PRISONERS/FUCK THE PRESS."

Old man on the bus

South Beach bus stop station about 10:30 a.m. on a Wednesday. Really too late to go to work, but Frank Harding, 75, isn't going to work. The clear morning sun flashes ruthlessly through the bus. A man, a suit-man, hurries to the bus, newspaper under left arm, flapping briefcase in the right hand, just makes the bus, breezing by the vertiginous green faces of the old farts in their seats grasping the seatback rails. Silent doors close and a swoosh into oblivion.

Plenty of empty seats. Too late for workers. This bus is filled with pastels and plastic bags. The suit-man plops down beside Harding. "Gorgeous morning, great for a walk on the beach, eh?"

The old man wears a khaki porkpie hat, baby blue polyester jacket over a yellow madras shirt. A Kodak camera hangs around his neck from a chromed metal chain. "I suppose," he said and looks steadily at the man through thick trifocals. "I'm going to my doctor."

"Oh, hope nothing serious."

"No, just the usual, heart, lungs, stomach, liver… but the brain's O.K."

"You're a photographer. That's one of the old Kodak Retinas, beautiful cameras."

"I dabble in it."

"Well maybe after the doctor you can catch the Man Ray exhibit at the Bass over on 22nd. That's what I'm thinking, if I had the day off."

"Yeah, but Man Ray was much more than a photographer, you know, painting, sculpture and geesh, just about everything. I know. I was in Paris before the war, just about the same time he was getting there."

"Military?"

"No, I was a lawyer at the time. But then, later, I was stationed in Paris as the war ended."

"What was Paris like then? Sartre at the Deux Maggots, poetry on coffee-stained napkins?"

"Yes, that too, but I was too young and full of beans to sit around cafés. But there were the girls. Oh my, the girls of Paris."

The old man looked at his reflection in the window. Blasts of sunlight. "That's when I met Claudia. Just an office girl, you know. She showed me Paris. I remember one time best, when we climbed up to the top of the Arc de Triomphe, all the way up. It's very cold and windy in March up there, and we were all bundled up, hat, beret, overcoats. You could see all the way past the Seine, and the Germans were gone. A strong gust blew the beret from her head. I remember her long dark hair stinging my face, and she, reaching over the ledge for the hopeless beret, reaching, reaching out — mon chapeau, mon chapeau, mon chapeau…"

He was quiet now.

"Did you marry her?"

"No. Then they sent me back to London and I met an English girl. Nice girl.

"And during the war?"

"I was drafted as a clerk typist. I was there, Battle of the Bulge, but never fired a gun."

The first of the Deco facades goes by. "My stop, sir. Good luck at the doctor. Enjoyed our conversation."

"Yeah, me too. Hey, I never liked Man Ray. Too goddamn modern, you know."

"Yeah, I know. Damn, I'm late." Silent doors closing behind him. Swoosh of the bus pulling out, disappearing in the glistening morning.

God Bless Joe Stalin

I'm sitting with Uncle Frank in his little South Beach condo for breakfast at his kitchen table drinking coffee, nibling at toast. To the left, above us, an open jalousie window directs an ocean breeze at us. The obituary page of the newspaper rests open.

Frank is mumbling something that I can't follow about Man Ray, then switches to the obituaries. "There's fifteen dead on the obit page today, and every one of them is younger than me. I'm a very old man," he says.

"You're a lucky old man. The alternative is not all that great. Ever think of that?" I said.

"Everything in this paper bores me. I've seen it all before. I've lived longer, much longer than anything that can ever happen. I've even outlived God. And there's another war..."

"Another war, Uncle Frank?"

"The war, the war."

"What war?"

"It's always the same war, godless destruction and death."

"War and death are the absence of God, but it doesn't mean there's no God." I'm egging him on a bit to get him going on a story. I haven't been a Christian since grade school, and I know he's a godless Commie.

"Or that there is a God. So why is He absent when they really need Him there?" he said.

"It's the absence of God in men's actions that leads to war."

"They say there are no atheists in the trenches. But during the war, I was still clinging to Stalin. You ever hear of the Battle of the Bulge, Jonas? Ever hear of it?"

"Yes, of course, end of World War Two."

"That's the closest I ever came to any sort of God. I was a terrible infantryman, the archetypal ninety-four-pound weakling and nearsighted, so they sent me to the rear with the cooks and the clerks to inventory fuel drums. I counted hundreds of fuel drums stacked to the sky. The weather had been bitter cold and overcast, but then after Christmas it cleared, and I heard the hum and rumbling and saw German planes darkening the sky. Then they opened up like pregnant frogs dropping guppies, hundreds of parachutes. The Germans were falling right on top of us."

"What the hell did you do? You prayed?"

"I panicked. Sweet Joseph Stalin protect me, I whined."

"You prayed to Joe Stalin?"

"That's what came to mind. I'm an atheist and a red. What else could I do? I guess it was some universal power of prayer because as they dropped, the German paratroopers saw they were landing right on our lines and thought they were doomed, and they dropped their weapons and waved their arms in the air surrendering as they touched ground. And the potato peelers and the clerk-typists marched all the captured German soldiers right into divisional headquarters."

"So how did that bring you closer to God?"

"Well I still pray all the time. Every one of those German soldiers wore a belt buckle engraved with the words *God With*

Us. That's why I couldn't find Him. I stuck with Joe Stalin."

"You know, they say Stalin was more of a monster than Hitler."

"Joe Stalin got a bum rap."

"Guppies don't drop from pregnant frogs, Uncle Frank," I said. "They hatch from eggs."

"Oy vey!"

Feeding the monster in Little Havana

Although there are no signs up yet identifying the new newspaper office on the strip mall, the man chained to the door spotlights the newsroom storefront for me. Only a Miamian would understand the visceral reaction against the Spanish language paper from the hardline exiles, incited by the Spanish language radio stations. They want the papers to actively push exile hatred of the Castro regime. Any normal attempt to cover Cuba is simply treason, and to see it in Spanish adds insult to injury. It's born-again Christianity against the devil.

In sharp contrast to the newsroom downtown, the Little Havana office is cramped and makeshift, with harsh bright colors on walls displaying the remains of travel posters. Nano Quintana, 39, a dwarf with male pattern baldness above black hair slicked back at the temples runs the bureau. Two-by-fours and unfinished plywood boards rest against the walls. Quintana's office, at one end of the room oversees activity through a wide now glassless window. A wooden board, once the private office door, protrudes from the window, resting on the horseshoe shaped copy desk, providing a convenient bridge for Quintana as he bounds the length of the plank landing atop the table.

The incessant clacking of three already obsolete Teletype machines pervades the room. Espresso coffee cups, take-out food boxes and stacks of newsprint cover the horseshoe shaped copy desk.

Two older men in short-sleeved guayaberas shouting at each other, waving pages of the Spanish language newspaper, ignore me as I walk in. The argument has to do with the Falkland Islands, a fucking stupid argument in Miami about islands in the South Atlantic. The Argentines were threatening to invade the islands, and the British promised to defend them. The problem now for a Spanish language paper, whether to call the islands by their Spanish name or their English name, each with proprietary political ramifications — which nation owned the islands — had no obvious solution. The English newspaper had decided to neutralize the quandary by calling them by both names — Falkland-Malvinas. The argument here, to use Malvinas first as in Malvinas-Falklands or just Malvinas, had ramifications, and the Cuban editors love the sub-levels of political and semantic intrigue. What appears to be a prelude to a fistfight erupts in laughter as another voice pipes in from behind three CRT monitors bunched at one end of the copy desk. "Fucking Argentines, always fucking everything up." As I settled into my new job, I realized that shouting, the usual method of communication in this newsroom, defined the importance of the subject at hand. Anything of note elicited a delightful argument.

"Just follow the English paper's orders on the fucking Malvinas," Nano says.

Quintana reminds me of a scaled down version of film director Carlo Ponti, Sophia Loren's husband, setting up a movie scene. The two editors — the news editor, Antonio

Contreras, 68, and Herminio Torquemada, 70, covering sports
— turn toward me. From behind the terminals an "hola" from
the translator Alberto Legrand, 65.

Nano, standing on the desk, sticks out his hand.

"Bienvenido a tu casa, Jonas. Welcome home. What do
you think of our copy flow arrangement... think I'll keep the
gangplank."

"Out of spite?"

"Nah, gives me a better view."

"That guy's been chained out there quite a while."

"New guy every day since we opened up, and they change
during the day. We give them coffee and a Cuban sandwich
for lunch."

"Where are the reporters' desks?"

"We don't have reporters, chico. We just translate the shit
from downtown."

"You've got a reporter now, chico. Give me a fucking desk."

Nano points his chin at an empty corner desk near the
window. El Jíbaro, the photographer, a Puerto Rican from New
York, sitting at the adjacent desk holds up a strip of negatives
to the window light. Campesinos in Puerto Rico proudly call
themselves jíbaros, and so does Roberto Corinto, 30.

"Watch out for the glass, man. On the chair. They threw a
brick through that window." El Jíbaro stands to his full lanky
height to greet me. His blue jeans are held up by a wide black-
leather belt clasped into place by a silver buckle bearing a red
hammer-and-sickle in bright relief.

"Careful with this guy," Nano says. "He's the only Marxist
Latino in Little Havana. Keeps a pint of Stoli in his desk."

"Actually, I'm really a Stalinist, man. Joe Stalin saved us
from the Nazis."

"Personally, I favor Trotsky, compañero, although my uncle agrees with you. But how the hell do you survive here?"

El Jíbaro reaches around his waist to the small of his back and pulls out a chunky blue-black revolver. "It's the gear, man, it's the gear. I only carry the best equipment. Smith & Wesson, six shots, 44."

"That's a fucking howitzer. Had to use it?"

"Not yet, man, and I hope I don't, but every motherfucker in the valley of the shadow knows I got it, and it'll blast a hole the size of a watermelon."

"I don't approve of that, and I don't know he carries," Nano says.

I let the box with my stuff from the downtown office drop to the desk, and Nano points back to Contreras, holding a ream of wire copy, and to Torquemada.

"That's the staff," Nano says, giving me the lowdown. Contreras, recently from the AP, is a great wire man, Nano says. They call him Contrarias, the devil's advocate on every issue, and he insists you're just looking at a ghost of the man who died in 1959. Then there's Torquemada — they call him Tercomada — who never changes his mind, no matter what. He still insists on using Cassius Clay instead of Muhammad Ali, but he knows Cuban sports history, man, better than anybody, and the exiles love him. Hiding behind the computers you'll find Legrand, the translator. He's totally insane, Nano says, Fidel fried his brain — just avoid him as much as possible — but he can machine gun any story into Spanish in a couple of minutes. Oh, and the malas-lenguas gossips say he's been after Laura, the wife of Manolo Rosales, the terrorist.

"Haven't seen your byline lately, Jonas," Nano says. "I like the way you write."

"Tight."

"Tighter than a rewrite man on a bender," Nano says.

"But after Salta Tigre, I couldn't write, not sure exactly why. I got back and couldn't write a word. I was impotent. Anything I could say seemed inadequate, irrelevant. I was a microbe."

"Just blocked, man. It happens."

"It's more than that, Nano. I haven't recovered from what happened to me in Salta Tigre, and now just the sight of the news-room downtown brings back a black hole in the jungle. I can't go back to that newsroom, ever. It just seems irrelevant now."

"What'll you do with your life?"

"Don't know. But I know nausea when I feel it."

"Well, I didn't expect to get a reporter, so anything I get is great, even a slightly damaged one. Maybe you'll write for me, man, in Spanish."

"You're not irrelevant Nano. Let's start that way, in Spanish, and see how it goes. But they said you needed a copy editor."

"Bullshit. They don't give a shit about what I need."

"I'll help you feed the monster."

Laura Rosales walks in at that point after leaving a buchito, a thimble-sized sip of black Cuban espresso, with the chained man at the door. A tall, formidable sight, high-heeled in tight black toreador pants and her trademark low-cut black blouse, Laura hands out a bouquet of tiny paper buchitos to the news-room staff congregating around her. She doles out the coffee like granting absolution and leaves, gracing Nano with a suffo-cating abrazo, jamming his head into her cleavage. "Tú eres mi enanito bello, corazón."

From the back, Legrand emits a soulful adios, "¿y mi cortadito, qué pasó?" blissfully ignored by Laura. "Inmetible," unbearable, she says to herself.

Still early, the newspaper dummies had only just arrived, Nano and I agree that a beer is in order. As we leave, I hear the beginning of another discussion that would go on for days — the availability of chicas in the pre-Castro paradise that pervaded their minds. "Por dos pesos, boquita, cosita, y culito," for two pesos you got lips, pussy and butt, said Legrand. "Tas loco," said Herminio, with emphasis on the loco, "Cincuenta centavos, mi hermano, cincuenta centavos," fifty cents, my brother, fifty cents. Contreras grabs the blank dummy sheets while Herminio rips the roll of photos from the AP Wirephoto printer.

The Little Havana Press Club

The last storefront anchoring the strip mall L —The Chévere Bar and Grill — belonged to a Costa Rican expatriate, José Villegas, 40, who was known in Little Havana as the bastard son of José Figueres, former president of Costa Rica. Several photos of the ex-president graced the mirror behind the bar, and José was his spitting image from the hooked nose down to the high-heeled boots he wore to rise from his five-feet-four stature. It was said that the Figueres family put him on a stipend to keep him in Miami.

José set the record straight from the beginning. He was delighted to see another Tico in the neighborhood, and it didn't matter that I wasn't gay, although he preferred that I sit away from the bar and next to a wall. That table soon became known as the Little Havana Press Club.

After a couple of weeks, the furor over the opening of a Spanish language edition died down somewhat although Miami's Cuban radio stations continued to castigate us over most articles, and they peppered their broadcasts with personal attacks against the writers. Jíbaro's .44 magnum was starting to make sense. I usually started my day listening to the screaming exiles on the air to find out what was going on en la sagüesera, the fast Cuban lingo way to say Cuban Southwest Eighth Street, the heart of Little Havana.

After putting the paper to bed one night, over my usual beer at Chévere's, to my amazement Manolo Rosales strolled up to my table with an easy gait that bellowed his Navy blazer.

"So, this is the Little Havana Press Club." Rosales sat down and looked me in the eye. I greeted him with, "what's the fucking problem, man," savoring the irony.

"You're still the problem, chico." He forced a smile. "No worry, Jonas. Just saying hello. I'll never understand how you managed to walk away from Salta Tigre. Both sides should have killed you.

"I guess they wanted me to tell the story."

"And you didn't."

"I don't like murderers telling me what to do."

He looked rested and perhaps a little grayer in the barlight. I imagined how it had ended at Las Pavas, with my uncles escorting him out of Turrialba.

"So, it's just no hard feelings, just like that," I said.

"Yes. I don't have time for that bullshit right now, and with Laura's café across the street we were bound to run into each other." Rosales said he had a couple of points to make and we probably wouldn't meet again. First, he wanted to thank me for standing up for Laura. The newspaper had run another more complimentary article focusing on the cultural importance of the small restaurants, labeling Laura's Café the go-to-place for ropa vieja and Cuban black beans. And second, he had a warning for me — Gabriela blamed me for Watson's death and would never let it go. In her black-and-white thought process, he said, the fact that I got out alive meant I was in league with the guerrillas. Also, for the first time, I began to understand Gabriela's power in the structure of the presidential office. The president seemed oblivious to her accumulation of influence with the military and his own security force. She was ordering assassinations and the president just let it happen. Rosales told me that the massacre at Salta Tigre that originally drew me to Guatemala was cooked up by her and Watson at the kitchen table in the Presidential Palace to draw more U.S. money and arms and to solidify Watson's influence in the Army.

"Gabriela is the new Guatemalan consul general in Miami. She's here, and I know I'm being followed around," he said. "And I'm sure she's on your tail too. She never forgets. If an ant bites her toe, she doesn't rest until it's squashed. She loved Watson and she blames you."

"And I never met the woman. I know that she's a black woman originally from Belize, but that's all."

"Well, she knows you. She's been with the President's family since childhood, and he's attached to her at the hip. But tell me one thing, just curious, why didn't you write anything about the firefight at Salta Tigre?" he said. "A lot of good men died. For what? Don't you have a fiduciary responsibility?"

"Fiduciary? That's a fancy word for a gunslinger."

"I was an English major at the University of Havana before the revolution."

"Well you should understand writer's block. I was numbed. Couldn't anchor myself and the events of those days were like an avalanche, beyond a news-story explanation. Left alone, it had more dignity. At a certain point I wasn't a witness, so involved in the Guatemalan death and squalor that had ripped me away from the American newspaper, by that time a distant entity, clean and antiseptic, so foreign to me that I couldn't comprehend it. When you walked into my aunt's house in Las Pavas, you decided you wouldn't kill them. I know you could have killed them all in a minute. That didn't make sense either. You too decided on a separate peace."

"You have something there, chico. Gabriela sent me there to kill you, and you weren't there. And in that big house, I realized it was over. My war was over when I couldn't recognize the enemy. That decision made me Gabriela's enemy." Rosales smiled, downed the beer, got up slowly and began to walk away, but turned for a moment looking at me, then turned again and was gone.

He was right, Gabriela was stalking us, and I didn't see Rosales again until weeks later, the night of the service at Reverend Núñez's Christian Church of Family Reunification.

———

As far as Bruton and the other suits downtown were concerned, the Spanish edition was born on borrowed time with a low horizon and a short-term existence. They gave it five years at best, rationalizing that Cuban immigration had peaked, the original exiles would have settled in and adopted English and their children would be American. With that prejudice firmly in place, and a tad of racism as well, they looked on the new bureau as a public relations effort to pacify the right-wing exiles and were unprepared to look at Little Havana as a viable news story. They were largely focused on a new flood of cocaine in Miami and the violence associated with Colombian drug traffickers. The Spanish edition had the opposite effect. It pissed off the exiles and spawned a mess of right-wing tabloids.

Nano had an irrepressible nose for news and a mother-in-law keeping him abreast of the important goings on in the sagüesera. Through her, he found out that Núñez's church pushed a single tenet, building a popular movement to allow more Cuban exiles to visit the communist island. It turned out that both governments liked the idea. Some of the more down-to-earth Cuban business leaders in Miami, among them the owner of the largest Chevrolet dealership in the city, Rosales's stepbrother, Daniel Schuster, were secretly negotiating with Cuban emissaries to open up the island to more family visitations. Helped along by Jimmy Carter's State Department, which saw the returning exiles as ambassadors selling the U.S. way of life in the Communist island, the movement thrived. The Castro regime, starved for foreign exchange, saw a unique opportunity for easy money and, who knows, perhaps an easing of the decades-long U.S. embargo. Those conversations became known as "the dialogue," and the Cuban exile participants became "dialogueros." A slew of right-wing groups sprouted during the dialogue, some of them deadly, about the same time the newspaper's new Spanish edition went to press.

I got the latest updates through Laura and Sonya, Nano's mother-in-law, both faithful congregants in Núñez's new Christian church in Hialeah. The minister and the congregation followed one guiding principle — allow Cuban exile families to return to Cuba to briefly reunite with loved ones and the travelers paid the church for the tours with good American dollars.

The English edition of the paper largely ignored my stories branding Núñez's church as just another exile bullshit fantasy until a fateful event blew their prejudices away. As other travel agencies selling family reunification tours opened for business, Havana Tours in Miami and another in San Juan, bomb threats became common. One early morning, an explosion shattered the Little Havana showroom of Schuster's Chevy dealership and a new gang, Omega 7, claimed responsibility. I reached out to Rosales who confirmed the story for me and he arranged an interview with Schuster.

———

Daniel Schuster sees two gigantic flags, one Cuban, one U.S., flutter over the cars in the lot of his Chevy dealership. The large plate-glass doors are closed. Schuster alone inside, in the back, waking from a siesta, stares into the mirroring image of the glass doors. A uniformed security guard holding an M-16 looks back at him. The huge flags dissolve into gigantic Nazi banners, swastikas billowing. The guard is now a Nazi officer turning, striding in strong deliberate steps through the gate of a concentration camp, through wintry desolation, specters in striped uniforms turn and follow him with their gaze as he slogs through, passing by the drab gray barracks buildings, entering a clinic. Patients in white metal beds line each wall. He walks through, glancing right to left, left to right, through a door — a middle-aged man in a white lab coat undressing a little boy, through another door – a man in a long white lab coat buggers a standing woman bent over an examination table. The woman turns holding her breasts, then reaching out with one hand, dirt slips through her fingers. A rolling ball of fire envelops the showroom.

———

Daniel Schuster was an impressive man. A child in the Nazi concentration camps during World War II, he survived the Holocaust and was brought to Havana sponsored by an aunt after the war. A Havana cop as a young man and having lived through Russian communism as a boy in Lithuania, he fled the Castro regime to Miami as soon as he could, falling into free enterprise heaven. As the CIA began to form an invasion force to overthrow Castro, he joined Brigade 2506 and landed on the beaches of the Bay of Pigs with his stepbrother Manolo Rosales and 1500 other hapless fighters only to cool his heels in a Cuban prison for 20 months until the Cubans traded them for American tractors. After Dachau, he said, the Cuban prison was just a small parenthesis in his life and he used all his survival skills to maneuver his way into the top tier of auto dealers in Florida.

The background as an exile patriot that helped propel him to business success in Miami clashed with his active support for family reunification and couldn't protect him after the exile radio stations branded him a dialoguero. Having survived the Nazi camps, where every action and reaction threatened to kill him, Schuster was impassive to bullying from the exile right wing. The image in his mind of his beloved aunt Esther welcoming him to Cuba was a permanent reminder of an obligation that could never be repaid, and she died without family, buried in a cardboard box with only Yitzhak Belman and a neighbor to say goodbye. Several other businesses suffered the rage of the radio stations and anti-dialogue terrorists — boycotts and bombs — as the viajes movement intensified but could not stop the wave of enthusiasm and seething demand among exiles to see their famlies in Cuba, if only for a few days. To sell the tours, the Cubans opened a Havana Tours travel office, using a Jamaican license, near the newspaper bureau right on Eighth Street. The Christian Church of Family

Reunification became the other tour agent. Soon, the huge cloth suitcases bound for Cuba, bursting with everything from medicines to Pilón and Bustelo coffee, jammed lines at Miami International Airport.

Leaks

Miami International Airport is like a frenetic Singapore, a foreign city-state with harsh laws and no appeal, and the way Armando Rocha, 55, sees it, you screw up once and the law freefalls on you mercilessly. Armando looks around as he walks, steadily sweeping the moving throng for any sign of danger, of possible interference as he, Nano Quintana, his son-in-law, and Huequín follow Sonya at a prudent distance. You never know when la vieja, as Armando calls his wife of thirty years, will pull a fast one, Armando says. As Cuba opens up to la comunidad, la vieja will travel often to the island to see her family. Sonya, 49, maybe an inch over five feet, wears her hair in a golden beehive. The high heels clicking down the crowded concourse don't elevate her as much as they tilt her forward. "We're already running late," Nano Quintana says, but they follow cautiously, not too close, as they approach the security checkpoint and push the enormous Cuba-bound suitcase forward as far as they can. Sonya leans toward the gate followed closely by Huequín as Armando and Nano begin their retreat, quietly.

Sonya's trips to Cuba are delivery expeditions. She's usually a caravan of one. Today she also guides Huequín along on his first trip back home to Güira de Melena. Huequín, a slight man in his seventies, has nurtured the thought of returning to Cuba for years, but he says he's sure Fidel has it in for him. Imagínate, Fidel thinking about this cretin, Sonya said. She has no patience for the delusional politics of exile. For her, only one thing matters — her family is hungry. The situation is clear, the action is obvious: go often and take back as much as you can pack in the huge cloth suitcase sold especially for the Cuban trips. They're not starving to death, she says, but they might as well be — hunger is also in the mind like a little worm, spinning incessantly.

Huequín means little hole in English. The way Armando tells the story, as a child Huequín would hide in holes. He felt safe and comfortable in a corner, in the fold of the tablecloth or in a closet. His dad would say, find el hueco and you'll find Huequín. Huequín was not convinced he should leave the protection of his cottage in Hialeah. He felt exposed when he thought about traveling to Cuba. But green dreams haunted him. He dreamed of the green mountains with palm trees sticking out, bending like lazy antennae over the bohíos, the rich red soil, and the moisture-laden breezes that seem to puff droplets in your face in the heavy green afternoons. O.K., he tells Sonya, next time, m'embullo, I'll be there with bells on.

And now they stand before a tall black woman in uniform. The alarm already stopped Sonya. "All this stuff hanging," the officer says. "You're some kind of Christmas tree." Armando shifts uneasily, not sure if they should recede or advance. "Coño, there she goes," he says.

"Cubans thank God for Christmas trees like me," Sonya says. And the strip begins. Barbie dolls, broaches, Bic shaving razors, a bag of Pilón coffee… "Why didn't you just pack this stuff?" the officer asks. A line is forming behind them as the goods pile up on the conveyor belt. Huequín stands to one side, his face taking a green tint. Finally, it all goes through.

"They don't know that over there you have to hide the stuff in your clothes or the Cubans steal it," Sonya tells no one in particular, but they can hear her clearly on the other side of the security area. Huequín, scrunching his shoulders, follows her pulling the Cuban suitcase. Finally, all you can see is the huge suitcase wobbling toward the gate.

———

Nano knows that following Sonya through MIA puts Armando in a nervous state that'll take days to wear off. He likes to start a job early, say 7 a.m., so he's already in a doubly bad mood. For him, life is about containment, building structures that withstand water pressure, and Sonya is more like natural gas, an uncontrollable explosive element he has never understood. Nano likes to help the old plumber from time to time. He loves the old stories of Cuba.

Now, they're working on a house Nano bought on Key Biscayne near the beach, which is where he's thinking he should be instead of pushing pipe in the house's crawlspace. But Armando, of course, won't let any comemierda come and do a lousy job and charge a fortune. "Hand me the Channel-Lock." Nano had already measured the work site and bought 30 feet of two-inch PVC pipe, 20 feet of three-quarter hot-and-cold PVC and a couple of hundred connectors. "Is this all we need?"

Armando just grunts as he slides into the crawlspace and Nano knows he'll measure the whole area again. Armando is a master plumber and Nano, the managing editor of the newspaper's new Spanish edition, is his helper today. Slightly under six feet, with long arms and big hands, Armando can work standing straight legged and bent over at the waist all day.

"That's the way we used to cut cane in Güira before Fidel," he says, "Strong back, carajo." They've been working together for a couple of days now, and Nano gets no respect. No offense, Armando says, he doesn't respect helpers. He needs them — he only has two hands and he needs four — but their capacity for fucking up is limitless. He even has less respect for Nano, he fondly tells him with a grin, since he's only 148 centimeters tall (about 4-feet 10-inches, but Armando likes to measure it out in centimeters) and a journalist with no honest dirt under his fingernails, some twenty years his junior, married to his daughter. "Look at Sonya," he says, "that's what's waiting for you." He usually finishes his sentences with comemierda, which literally means, "shit eater" but a better translation is "asshole." Sometimes, for added emphasis, he'll say comemierda carajo. Carajo means "prick," but he just uses it as special punctuation like an exclamation mark at the end of a sentence. Carajo does not have nearly the power of coño, a female force enveloping and squeezing the crap out of a chaotic universe.

Now he's fretting about Huequín. He doesn't worry about Sonya, who swings tres pares de cojones, three sets of balls, he says, but Huequín is a very sensitive man. "It's hard the first time you go back to Cuba. The emotion of the return is overwhelming, traumatizing."

Way back, Huequín was his assistant. Armando gave him his first job when Huequín began exile life in Miami. But Armando told him straight out, go work as a janitor, "You'll never make a plumber, comemierda." Aside from a certain gentleness that could be mistaken for hesitance, or worse, a slightly effeminate shyness, Huequín possessed a peculiar characteristic that at first amused Armando no end, but which later became an annoyance. One of the middle toes on Huequín's left foot began to grow when he left Cuba, reaching a length some two inches beyond his other toes. Armando said, showing on a piece of PVC exactly how long it stuck out. The long toe was flexible, but he couldn't fold it. It stuck out. And according to Huequín, no doctor would cut it off. Huequín had to cut a hole in his shoe. "I don't know how he grew the toe," Armando says, "It was a medical mystery. Huequín would flap it around, cut it on something and bleed on the job. "I'm gonna shoot it off," Huequín would wail, but he never did, and he got a job as a school janitor.

Under the house, on their backs looking up at the underside of the floor, which is crisscrossed neatly by new PVC pipe, Nano's head rests on Armando's shoulder as they glue up another joint. The glue leaves yellow patches on Nano's hands, and the smell makes him sick. Armando thrives on it. "Keeps that water locked in." As he concentrates on the pattern of future flow and effluence, much like a hunter stalking game, he begins to hum, and then he tells how he felt the first time he returned to Cuba, a sign he's feeling better now when he starts the stories. "It was traumatic, carajo." They finish the water supply pipes and turn on the water main to test the joints as Armando tells the tale of the death of Benito Remedios.

At 25, Armando worked as the chauffeur for a rich man, Benito Remedios, in Güira de Melena, their hometown about 50 miles south of Havana. "Back in '55," he says, "Benito owned more than 100 farms, but never said he owned more than 99 farms (I don't want 100, Benito would say, if I own 100 farms, the government will take one away) growing pineapple, sugarcane, everything, 120 trucks, and he was the elected representative for the Güira district." Armando's dad also drove a truck for Benito, and on Election Day, he would pick up voters, give each one of them a peso and take them to the polls. It's the best way, Benito always said, because that way he didn't owe them anything after he got elected. Benito was a self-made man, a hard man with a bad temper, with as many enemies as friends. He started out with Armando's dad in the hard old days, hauling sugar cane bagazo with one ox cart. But he made it. "Le ronca el mango," Armando says, that's something like "amazing." When Armando went back to Guira in '79, his brother Corucho took him over to Benito's old motor pool. Once, all the shiny trucks lined up there, neatly, at a 45-degree angle, ready to pull out and go. Now all you could see was the cannibalized rusting remains of maybe half a dozen trucks. "¡Coñó!" he says, with a particularly Cuban stress at the end of the word. Armando uses it at the beginning of a sentence, as an opening exclamation mark. "That moved me," he says, "brought it all back. I know how Huequín feels." He walked slowly through the truck grave-yard and stopped, he says, speechless, before the remains of Benito's Buick convertible. He leaned on Corucho. The four-door white beauty, the one he used to pump into overdrive, the one Benito died in. "Hecho mierda," he said, "a piece of shit." Only a doorless, burned-out hulk remained like a huge empty skull. "Why trash that beauty? Maybe they burned it in a fit of revolutionary rage."

Armando senses a water leak somewhere. Nano doesn't hear it, but Armando shushes him and turns over, crawling to the edge of the house. He hears it and sees it, but he has to feel it to really understand it. He reaches up until it drips on his hand, and he gently pulls a little on the plastic pipe. A nail protruding from the floorboards had snuggled right into the cold-water pipe. They have to cut the piece off, pull it out and start over. Nano later in life will remember that moment, when typos on the front page demand a remake at 2 a.m. His back aches and the muscles around his neck are tight and sore. He can't lift his arms. But he has to.

"It was a beautiful car," Armando continues in stride. "Smooth, quiet '48 in-line eight, looked like a creamy white swan on the road. Benito would sprawl in the back, one leg on the back of the front seat, the other resting fully on the back seat and would tell me to move it, move it. Haul ass goddamit." The big Buick would make it to Havana in less than an hour. Only Armando was allowed to drive for Benito, except that one day. Benito's oldest son, Pepe, kept a woman about an hour's drive from Güira and that day he drafted Armando. Benito was upset when he was called to Havana without his favorite driver, they later told Armando. He didn't like to travel without his best driver. Armando and Pepe were on the road back to Güira when they heard the news on the radio — Benito Remedios was shot dead on the corner of Reina and Águila in Havana.

"Como lloré. I cried at his wake," Armando said. "If I had been driving him instead of Ambrosio, it wouldn't have happened, carajo." Now they're finishing the drainpipes, the big two inchers, and they're spreading enough glue to kill subterranean termites clear to Little Havana. Embedded in the crawlspace dirt, bundled like lovers, they grip and shove the pipes into place. "See, in those days the traffic cop controlled the stoplights from a little kiosk in the middle of the intersection, and Ambrosio parked illegally right in front of the cop while he waited for Benito. Naturally, he got a ticket. This car belongs to Representative Benito Remedios, he told the cop. I don't give damn if this is Batista's car, the cop said, and Ambrosio, said comemierda, and just then Benito appeared, and Ambrosio handed him the ticket as he opened the car door, and Benito smashed his fist into the cop's face, and the cop went down, and Benito started to kick him (he wore yellow calfskin shoes, those baggy pants and a white long-sleeved guayabera), and the cop pulled his pistol and shot him from the ground right through the heart, and Benito dropped dead into the back seat of the Buick."

They pulled out of the crawlspace. It was late afternoon now, and the breeze thankfully had swept the glue fumes away. They sat together just resting. "I used to get traffic tickets every day," Armando said, "but I never showed them to Benito. I knew Benito would explode. I just tore them up and threw them away. Nobody ever came around looking for a Representative to pay a lousy parking ticket." Just then a joint on the cold-water pipe blew. Water poured out of the crawlspace. It was like the goddam house pissing on them. Nano shut the main and they slithered back under the house. "Years later, I ran into that cop right here in Miami," Armando said. He was a waiter at La Carreta over on Calle Ocho. "Hey, you're the man who shot Benito Remedios, I told him. "Please don't talk about it," he said. "You know what it means to kill a man?" He wasn't angry, an old man now. That moment, me cagó la vida, fucked my whole life, he said. He was lucky Batista didn't just have him shot right away; maybe it was because Benito had enemies too, and then the waiter languished in prison even though it was self-defense and later even in exile people still hated him for shooting Benito. "I'm sorry it happened to him and to me, too," he said. Armando wiped the newly cemented joint and waited a moment. No drip. They pull themselves out of the crawlspace and stretch out, Armando to his full stature, gratefully reaching up to the heavens and Nano, emulating him, stretches to his full height, just above the plumber's waist.

———

Two weeks later Sonya and Huequín are back, and she's pissed at Huequín. He's behind her, pulling the huge empty Cuban suitcase. At first, all she says is "Comemierda." Later, they drop off Huequín and hear the whole story.

After clearing security, Sonya is still upset at the black security guard's comment about the Christmas tree. She would never forget that insult and would mention it every time she went to Cuba after that. Then she jams into the window seat next to Huequín and rips her pantyhose. When she stops fuming and catches her breath, she notices that Huequín doesn't look well. As the plane jets out of Miami, he goes into a trance, staring ahead without blinking. Sonya rings for the stewardess. I think he's sick, she says. The stewardess looks at the little man and asks him to move his left foot, which rests slightly askew in the aisle with the long toe sticking out through a hole in the neat leather oxford. Huequín doesn't move. The pretty young woman leans forward and touches Huequín's face. Señor, señor, she says. He doesn't move. Then Sonya and the stewardess smell shit.

Alabao says Sonya. They unbuckle Huequín's seatbelt and the two women lift him up and half drag him to the lavatory.

They rest him against the sink in the cubicle and Sonya pulls down his pants. Carajito, she mutters, yo no le limpio el culo. They plop him down and jam the door shut. It's an hour flight to Havana. Huequín stays in the tight enclosure the whole trip and recovers just as they're landing. He bangs on the door. I feel fine, chévere, he tells Sonya.

"Comemierda," she says.

The Church of Family Reunification

María Osorio, a slim athletic figure in a red pantsuit and black patent-leather high heels that click smartly on the marble tile floors, high steps into the glittering glass Flagship Bank on Miracle Mile in Coral Gables. Her gait betrays a slight limp as she enters the bank and talks to a clerk who checks her identification and leads her to the safe-deposit-box vault. They withdraw a large metal drawer and the clerk takes it to a small room, puts it on a table and leaves her alone. María opens the box and removes a straw purse. Under it, a disassembled Ingram Mac-10 automatic machine pistol is nestled next to several packets of hundred-dollar bills, a silencer and two loaded clips. It all fits neatly in the purse. Outside the bank, she puts the top down on a baby-blue Mercedes 350 convertible and aims for Little Havana to an interview with Jonas Harding.

Sitting behind a high, massive counter at the Havana Tours travel agency, María looks up to see Harding backlighted by the light streaming through the plate-glass door. He looks taller than she remembers him, but now there's no question about it — Harding is Miguelito's priest.

"I'm Jonas Harding."

"Un placer."

He sees the scars on her left wrist. A black and white memory flash of her hands cleaning his eyes crosses his mind, and he immediately looks up at her eyes. "I've heard that you work directly for the Cuban government."

"You get right to the point, don't you? No, we're a Jamaican company with offices in New York and Havana and now Miami."

"But the money goes directly to Havana, right?"

"Not directly. We process it and deduct our commissions of course."

"Of course." His face burning, he looks away from her.

"You know, the fee covers everything except lodging. The members of the exile community returning to the homeland are expected to stay with their relatives. That's the whole point, anyway, right?"

"The distinguished members of the community used to be just plain gusanos. Remember?"

"It's family, Mr. Harding, family."

It's the dollars, ma'am, the dollars."

———

Harding walks past the chained protester into the newsroom, obviously in a daze, trying to piece it all together. He knows her — the Cuban guerrilla fighter in Salta Tigre. But what to do with that knowledge? Its only part of the puzzle.

The chained man shouts out as Harding walks past him. "Hey, man. Don't look at me! I don't like your fucking face."

"No more buchitos for you, asshole."

Harding plops down at his corner desk. El Jíbaro appears holding a batch of black and white photographs. "The Cuban government is running the fucking travel agencies," Harding says.

"Cool, man. But so what y qué? As soon as the commies make some money everybody's pissed off."

"It's fucking news, man, that's what. That's what we do, right?"

"You don't give a fuck," says Jíbaro.

"This is different now. I'm working for Nano."

"O.K. Now you give a fuck."

"We're in a cold war with Cuba, a total embargo, and they're right here under our fucking noses running a travel agency in Little Havana."

"Hey, watch out man, you're getting into this story and there's no turning back." El Jíbaro picks up a motorized Nikon and fires off a fusillade of shots at Harding. "Can you prove it?"

"Maybe there's proof at the Havana Tours office," Harding says.

"Know anybody inside?"

"Yes and no."

"What the fuck does that mean?"

"Forgetaboutit."

"Only one way to find out what's inside," says Jíbaro.

"What's that?"

"Get inside."

El Jíbaro drives a Chevy station wagon down a narrow alley and pulls up behind the strip mall at the back door of the Havana Tours office. The office is closed and dark. Harding leaves the car, goes to the door and then spots a jalousie window with the bottom slat missing. El Jíbaro comes around and boosts him up. He finds the latch and the window swings open into a small lavatory. He moves slowly through a narrow hall, into the darkened main office and approaches the filing cabinet.

"Hello, padre, I've been expecting you."

Harding whips around wide-eyed and spots her in a corner half lit by street-light filtering through the front window, aiming the Mac-10.

"Careful with that thing. They say the Mac-10 goes off on its own."

"Before we go any further let me warn you that this is the new improved version of the Ingram Mac-10, smaller, lighter and even fitted with a silencer it's capable of firing 30 rounds in less than two seconds and you know I can use it. Right?"

"Salta Tigre."

"Salta Tigre." María moves behind the counter, facing Harding.

"Absolutely. But, I'm counting on one thing."

"What's that?"

"You pulled my ass out of that hole in Salta Tigre, maybe you won't want to blow me away now... maybe you're a little sentimental."

María stifles a laugh, "Hardly. Miguelito saved your ass. You were just another corpse to me. Question is, what kind of priest are you now, padre, which denomination?"

A brick smashes through the plate-glass window followed by a Molotov cocktail exploding against the counter. Protected momentarily by the counter, they scamper out through the hall, and finding the back door locked they leap into the lavatory, escaping through the window as the entire office is engulfed in flames.

Harding and María squirm face down in the street, his right arm over her shoulders. El Jíbaro kneels beside them, gun in hand. Behind them the small travel agency building burns brightly. She turns over to look at the fire, pressing the Mac-10 to her breasts.

———

In her apartment, María sits at a small kitchen table while Harding cleans the bloody scratches on her face and arms.

"My turn, now."

"Your turn, now."

María and Harding nurse short drinks sitting across from each other, over a bottle of Stoli vodka. Still shaken by the firebombing, they gaze vacantly at the glasses, then hesitantly at each other. Harding focuses on her eyes, clear blue even in the dim light of the apartment.

"I like El Jíbaro."

"No bullshit with him. I guess you recognize a fellow traveler."

"He's all talk, romantic talk. Doesn't know what it's about."

"Ration cards, long lines, boredom, mind control."

"That's all meaningless. It's a war. It's a never-ending war, a war for self-respect, a war for everything. The war."

"What about the political prisoners, the torture and executions."

"They're all bloody battles in the war, battles in miniature. We're all in the same fucking war. You're in it, and you don't know it. I was tortured in prison, too. They were going to kill me, too. No. Nothing's right. Not then, not now."

"How long were you locked up?"

"A few months. A year. You lose track. They never tell you. Until Fidel rolled into Havana."

"How do you come back from that? I mean, how do you go through torture and waiting for execution and then come back out still a human being?"

"Compression."

"Compression?"

"Just because you're in prison, because they trapped you, because they mutilate you, that doesn't mean you stop thinking. Even after they break you, you come back around to what you were. But time stops. Everything intensifies, compresses, years become months, months days, days hours and you go with that until time stops altogether, and then you give in to an interminable present."

"But sure death, the firing squad..."

"It becomes part of the compression. In normal life, you know you'll die eventually, and you have to learn to deal with that — you find some meaning."

He pours more Stoli.

"Waiting for execution is not much different, only it doesn't exist in normal time. You're in that never ending now, time stops. The meaning of things doesn't change. You still fear death, the unknown, but you deal with it like you always did."

Harding looks at her eyes, downs his drink and reaches for her scarred wrist. Her hand is a small woman's hand, but calloused, hard; the nails are clear and plain, trimmed back, rounded on tapered fingers.

"These hands give you away. They're not travel-agent hands."
María pulls her hand away.

"Should I stay here tonight?" he says.

"Couldn't do that, even with a priest and the Mac-10 for protection. There's a lot to sort out."

"Then, I'd like to repeat the statement now."

"What statement?"

"I've heard you work directly for the Cuban government."

María lowers her head. Her hair falls over her face, then she half-glances up at him through her hair.

"Why didn't you ever write anything about Salta Tigre?"

"The paper demoted me, and I said fuck you to them all."

"Bullshit. I can't believe that."

"Yes, it is bullshit. I couldn't write. I left something in that hole in Guatemala. Part of myself. It's strange. I found something terrifying there. I found it and I left it all in the same instant."

"I understand."

"You do? How can you?"

"I also found and left, in prison. Did you see it, or did you just feel it?"

"It was intimate — we were bound together, but you pulled me out and I never want to see it again. I guess that's why I didn't write — the fear of seeing it again. I didn't want to linger in Salta Tigre."

"Are you afraid now?"

He reaches for her hand. His finger traces the scars on her wrist.

"And this? This is what you found and lost?"

"Yes, but it's not gone. It's still with me. I was only a student and didn't know much, but Batista's police tortured me, made me tell names and where to find them."

And…"

"They killed them, all of them."

"But this," Harding still holding her wrist.

"Yes. You're right. This I did to myself. I wanted to hurt myself, to punish myself for telling, and I never wanted to forget that the man who cut and broke my leg and clavicle had numbers tattooed on his chest.

"Ever find him?"

"Yes, in Guatemala."

"What happened?"

"You happened. You interfered. And you're still in the way. An impediment."

"An impediment, that's me. Always an impediment."

"After the firefight at Salta Tigre, I just barely made it back to Honduras."

"And the boys."

"Dispersed. But Miguel stayed. We buried him near there."

"I'm sorry. He saved my life."

"Yes, and paid a price, but the rest of us, we always disperse."

"Me too. I dispersed too."

"Remember, I have a job to do here, and you're in the way. You have to go now."

"Will I see you again?"

"I don't know. You're a problem. You're not dead. You're not just another corpse in the jungle, and that puts me at risk. What are you now, padre? I have to think about that."

"You can trust me, María," he says and he feels the tightening of a bond first tied in Salta Tigre.

"I don't even trust María, padre," she says.

———

In the Little Havana newsroom, Nano summons his crew up to the gangplank to plan the coverage of the big event at Núñez's Church of Family Reunification. Along with Havana Tours, the preacher will announce a special reunification mission to Cuba that will hold services on Havana's Plaza de Armas. Both Sonya and Laura are attending the service in the Hialeah warehouse, Nano says, and a huge attendance is expected.

"Downtown asked us to cover it. Harding writes the story," Nano says, darting a slightly askance glance in Harding's direction wondering if he can trust the damaged reporter to cover it properly given that he's still suffering from post-traumatic stress. "Jíbaro shoots the scene keeping in mind that he's covering for all editions and has an earlier deadline."

"Coño, I know that," El Jíbaro says.

"So you'll have to get out of there fast," Nano says.

"Claro, man. We expecting trouble?"

"Demonstrators probably already there. Cops all over the place. I wouldn't carry that piece in there if I were you," Nano says. "Harding, write up the background to the story and leave it with Contreras. That way he can have it translated into English and if you can't get back in time, call in the lede and he can smooth it down."

———

Outside a large converted warehouse in Hialeah in the early evening, police cars, lights flashing, separate a crowd of demonstrators from the building. Inside, about a hundred of the faithful, mostly middle aged and elderly women, sing and sway waving their arms to bombastic liturgical music.

María Osorio and several Miami and Hialeah politicians and businessmen occupy the front row. Manolo Rosales and

Laura are in the second row, accompanied by Sonya. Harding finds a seat behind them, near Manolo.

Núñez's bodyguards scan the audience from each side of the stage. Uzi submachine guns hang from their shoulders as Núñez swings his obese figure before a chorus of women wearing Cuban flags, banging on tambourines, sticks and maracas. The music quiets down as Núñez raises his arms and lowers them, silencing the audience. Parishioners are still walking in, looking for seats.

Núñez stares at his congregation, silently fixing them in place like a bullfighter before the kill, his gaze enveloping the whole audience, then starting slowly, his voice rises steadily to a frenzy.

You carried your cross.

Amen.

All the way from Oriente and Santiago and Havana...
Sí. Sí. Sí...

...you didn't complain, you didn't cry, you suffered in silence... from Havana.

Amen, brother, amen...

Your sons in Cuban prisons suffering alone, alone, alone and your sick and dying parents crying out your names from over there, over there, gone forever, from Havana...

Oh, Jesus, Lord Jesus...

And you suffered in silent prayer. Afraid, afraid. Afraid of what? Of politicians, all of them, all colors, all stripes, of men with guns and bombs in the darkness of the lonely night. They love their wars because YOU do their suffering.

Amen, brother. Amen! Amen!

But Jesus heard that prayer. Who heard? Who heard that prayer?

Jesus. Jesus heard.

And what did he hear? What did Jesus hear?

Havana.

Hallelujah.

Havana.

Family, Family, Family, Family reunification!

Hallelujah!

Family!

Hallelujah. Havana. Hallelujah!

María looks around, bemused with mocking eyes, smiling at the congregation now silent after the crescendo. Then she spots Rosales behind her. *Hola, Manolo*, she says to herself. Her training guides her gaze around the room, measuring the faces, and fixes to her left on a little man in a dark brown wool suit with a pattern of yellow pinstriped squares standing in the aisle leaning against the wall, sweat wetting his face, lifting a Smith & Wesson .357 magnum from under the left flap of his open jacket, aiming it, too large in his fists, away from her and directly at Harding. Harding, looking toward the stage, stares at Núñez as the preacher wraps up his sermon, trying to gauge the man's motives, which appear more connected to the CIA than to Jesus. Then Harding's neck snaps forward as Rosales shoves him away, uttering one word, *maricón*, and fires at the gunman, hitting him squarely in the face, and as if choreographed in a ballet, Rosales spins around to check on Laura as a burst of sustained firing from Núñez's bodyguards strikes his chest in an explosion of blood. The screaming congregation storms out of the warehouse and before Laura can react,

177

María falls on Rosales, pulling on his shirt, pressing on his chest as if trying to stem the bleeding. Captured by El Jíbaro for all editions, María Osorio's face, tears streaming, remains the last thing before Rosales's eyes.

———

Harding, Contreras and Torquemada sit at the rounded end of the copy desk. Nano on the gangplank facing them, holds Harding's copy.

"Downtown already has the copy, but what about the guy Rosales blasted?" Nano says, looking at Harding.

"He had a gun but never got a shot off. Cops aren't talking beyond that. We'll have to follow up tomorrow with the witnessses we can identify."

"About a hundred people there?"

"They scattered when Rosales fired his gun. And then Núñez's gorillas went crazy; miracle they didn't hit the people running out."

"So the story the cops are telling is that Rosales tried to shoot Núñez, but what about the other guy, doesn't make sense at all. Where's Núñez?"

"In protective custody for now."

"Maricón, maricón. That's all the hero said," Nano says.

"Well, I heard it. He was right next to me, and the cops also confirmed that."

Contreras raises his voice, "We can't print that."

"That's what the man said," Harding says.

"He's a hero in Miami, and that's not what a hero says before he dies, his last words," says Contreras.

"He's a fucking mercenary killer," Harding says.

"Cocksucker. That's what it means, cocksucker," says Tor-quemada. "You want the community to see that in tomorrow morning's paper over Cheerios? Cocksucker?"

"It's not about Rosales, Jonas. Just printing the word maricón is an insult to the community," says Contreras.

"And that's because it's not in the fucking dictionary of the fucking Royal Academy of the fucking Spanish language?" says Harding. "Fuck the community. Fuck you. It is about Rosales. I'm just quoting Rosales and the fucking cops."

"O.K, O.K, maricón stays in the story. Hey, let's wrap this up. We're on deadline. Close the goddamn paper," says Nano.

"What about Jíbaro's shots," says Harding.

"Well, a lot of discussion with downtown about that. The shot of Rosales dead with the Cuban woman like on top of him is fantastic, but you know, they had to debate it, too graphic, but they did play it inside, not page one."

"And us?"

"Front page."

"They know?"

"They'll see it over Cheerios with cocksucker," says Nano.

Harding leaves the news meeting driven by an unabating need to hold María. He knew the shooter — another soldier in Gabriela's army, on a mission to kill Rosales and probably dispose of the troublesome reporter as well. The little Mayan and his clones inhabited his nightmares in all their incarna-tions — sockless in Ramírez's home, the chess player in the Guatemala City hospital, half-buried in Chevo's backyard. He wondered how to tell María the story. Who knew the bound-aries of Gabriela's hate and lust for revenge? Gabriela's reach had brushed María too. María was involved, maybe even in danger. Harding pictured the man, sure that like the other sicarios, he wore no socks. A man like that would be virtually untraceable, and the Miami police would never identify him or understand his motive. He remained the footnote to a long story, hanging from a spider's gossamer thread that dropped off a kitchen table in Guatemala's Presidential Palace, spinning through an obscure Mayan village, murdering Ramirez's family, spinning sticky tendrils through Costa Rica and Havana and now weaving a web in Miami that killed Rosales and trapped Núñez and his Hialeah Church of Family Reunification.

———

"I'm glad you came back," María says.

Sitting at the kitchen table, her hair wet from a shower, her hands trembling just enough to be noticeable as she cleans the disassembled Mac-10 methodically. "What the fuck happened in that weird church?"

"They wanted to kill Rosales and me too, probably."

María's fingers rubbing oil on the stamped metal sides of the gun.

"But why, why there, they who?"

"It's a hangover from Guatemala, Salta Tigre. They were stalking Rosales. He told me that a few weeks ago and told me to watch out, they'd be after me too. I'm guessing he just followed us there, into the church and saw us together."

"You knew Rosales?"

"Yes. It all started with Salta Tigre. I was in Guatemala City to write a story about the village massacre. They assassinated Ramírez while I was there, and I met him in Ramírez's home, blood still wet. He ran security for the Guatemalan president who arranged for me to get to Salta Tigre, to confuse the story of Ramírez's death, to cover up the Army's role in the village massacre, probably to kill me… and you were there. They didn't expect that."

"It was Rosales. Rosales was the man who tortured me in Havana."

"Rosales?"

"I located him in Guatemala, but then the firefight at Salta Tigre ended my mission. In the end, I guess we all had an appointment in Miami."

"That sonofabitch who cut you up in that Cuban prison was Rosales?"

"It took me years to track him down, but I found his foster mother in Havana. Over time, Esther told me a lot. She was proud of both her sons, but afraid of Manolo's temper. She raised him like one of her own. The other one sells cars here in Miami. Nice lady. We would go walking on the Malecón."

"You can have some peace now."

"Peace? Maybe that comes around. Right now I just feel robbed, bitterness at having been robbed. I wanted to see the tattoo I told you about, the number, eau de cologne, on his chest, but it was blown away. I was robbed of that."

"Now, what do you do about it all, the trips to Cuba?"

"About me, the less you know the better. Just being near you puts me in danger. and I put you in danger, you know. We're both back in that black hole now."

"I should write about it, and you should stop me from writing about it."

"The cops will come around. The cover for the mission was blown away with Rosales. Nothing I can do about it. I have to disperse. Hit and run — that's how I do it."

"What about Havana? They'll want an accounting."

"You don't need to know about Havana."

"I know more than I want to know, more than I'll ever write about, but all that comes along with you, María, and I'm glad you came along, María..."

"Can you believe that no one really looked at me? Not even Núñez, not even Rosales."

"I'll be writing that the tour money goes straight to Fidel."

"I don't care. Núñez is still alive and the idea of trips to Cuba is so ingrained now that it'll never stop. And Fidel is releasing political prisoners. That's all. That was my job. I don't give a fuck about the rest of it."

"Come here." He hugs her. Lifts her fingers to his mouth, the smell of the oily Mac-10.

"Jonas, I want to know what you found in that black hole in Guatemala."

Explosions as he falls into the darkness. Jonas is five years old. Carlitos pulls Jonas's pants down his legs so he can't run. Behind them a quiet figure strapped into a child's highchair moves sometimes. Now, Jonas on his stomach, his face pressed against the wood floor, the wood grain in his eyes, the dust blowing with his breath, Carlitos heavily on top of him. A door opens a crack of light to the outside. Jonas stares at the edge of the door. "It hurts."

"Sure it hurts. Hurts me, too."

Carlitos pushes heavily into him. "You won't tell, will you?" Carlitos keeps the door open a crack so he can see who's coming. Jonas stares at the edge of the door. It hurts, Jonas says. Of course it hurts, Carlitos says. If it hurts you, imagine how much it hurts me. Finally, Carlitos rolls him over. You won't tell will you, he says, pressing his forearm against Jonas's throat, pushing too hard so the push goes deep into his chest and he chokes, puking a little and he realizes now that at that moment Carlitos considered killing him. Just a little more pressure. Someone passes by, a shadow past the crack of the door. Mira, Carlitos says, lifting him from the floor, carrying him to the back of the room where the silent figure rocks in the highchair. She told my mother and this is what happened to her, he says. He raises Jonas and pushes his face into the chest of a woman who sits legless strapped to the chair, a rag tight around her mouth. Instead of a face and arms, Jonas sees giant lobsters weaving air the way the fishermen lined them up on the Avenida Central for the holidays, and she reaches for him with claw hands, making sounds — he heard them now — deep grunting sounds. He heard himself cry to himself — no soy yo, no soy yo. And he ran and ran and would never tell anyone anything, not even himself, because Carlitos would turn him into a monster if he ever did. And he hears them again, sounds, deep groaning sounds as they pull him from the fissure into the fading afternoon light, coughing and snorting dirt, his burning eyes shut, aware only of a distant, echoing locomotive that dissolves into María's face shouting, "Open your eyes..."

Harding slowly opens his eyes to María's face. She holds his face and kisses him. He brings her wrist to his lips. For the first time, they look at each other directly, intensely, as if what had separated them had just vanished. He kisses her face and the hollow of her throat. In bed, he kisses her naked body, working down, his lips caressing the old cuts on her back and the deep scar running down her left thigh.

———

Harding elbows his way through a crowd. A dozen demonstrators swing a large banner that reads "Maricones." Two of the demonstrators sit on the sidewalk, chained to the doors of the newspaper office. A disheveled Laura chants along with the marchers.

"Maricones. Maricones."

Nano sits on the horseshoe copy desk. In front of him, El Jíbaro and Contreras. Harding joins them.

"Hola, maricones," Harding says.

"They're demonstrating downtown too. More than a thousand subscriptions cancelled."

"All because of me," says Harding.

"And me," says Nano, "Bruton said you're fucking insane, but that he expected more from me."

"You'll be selling papers in Little Havana all your life, you little shit," says Harding.

"They're planning a huge funeral rally at the original CIA training site for the Brigade in the Everglades."

"Bury Rosales in the Glades?" says El Jíbaro.

"Ashes, man, they'll scatter the ashes at night, this Sunday."

"How do we get in and out of that in time for deadline?"

"Chopper. I need the film way ahead of deadline."

"What happens when the chopper doesn't show?" says El Jíbaro.

"Cheerful comemierda, aren't you?" says Nano.

"I just know how it goes in Little Havana."

"O.K., I'll have a motorcycle messenger waiting outside the camp for the film. Then you call in the story. That's your backup."

———

Daniel Schuster pushes past the marchers and the chained demonstrators crowding around the entrance to the downtown newspaper building. Bruton and Rosenfeld pore over a newspaper in Bruton's office as Schuster leans in through the doorway. Mabel spots him and raises a warning hand, but Schuster walks in.

"Have you seen that demonstration outside? I don't think you guys are getting the message," says Schuster.

"We're used to it," says Rosenfeld. "They're getting to be a habit. Dan, do we owe you money or something? I thought the paper paid cash for the delivery trucks.

"I just want to remind you that the Orange Bowl committee meets next Monday...don't forget. And, by the way, that story Harding wrote in today's Spanish edition really insulted the community in a big way. That's why they're out there."

"We have a dead mercenary. He was about to murder Núñez. Pretty straightforward reporting."

"Not in the Spanish edition. It's not straightforward in Spanish. Nothing is straightforward in Spanish." Schuster's face trembles. The other two men, cool in light-blue button-down Oxford shirts and power ties, look calm, professional.

"Look, I have something to tell you. I didn't want it to interfere with the work I was doing with the Dialogue, but Rosales is my foster brother. We were raised together in Cuba, fought in the Bay of Pigs together and suffered in a Cuban prison together. A Cuban patriot. You treated him like dreck."

"Jesus Christ Dan, so sorry for your loss, but we didn't treat him. He was about to shoot Núñez. He was responsible for atrocities in Guatemala, and they kicked him out. He has a history and that's what we reported."

"What about the other shooter? Never mind. We'll honor Manolo this weekend at the old Brigada training camp in the Glades. But that's no longer the point."

"What's the point?" says Bruton.

"Harding's stories on the trips to Cuba are inflaming the community. You can't ignore those people out there forever," says Schuster.

"Jesus Christ, Dan, you know all this better than anyone," says Bruton.

"Look, I thought it would be good for the community at first, and I said so. I was thinking of my own stepmother. But I didn't go to Havana with the dialogueros."

"I guess you didn't expect to be firebombed," says Rosenfeld.

"Both countries agreed on this," says Bruton. "There's a lot of resistance and antagonism about the trips, Dan, but all the same, thousands of exiles want to go visit. What about them? We've been reporting on this all along. You know that."

"Yes, but not in Spanish. In Spanish you have to be more careful with nuances," says Schuster. "You don't have to emphasize that hundreds of millions of dollars are headed to Fidel's hands, and you're giving him free advertising. That's treason to the community out there. To them you're keeping motherfucking Fidel in power."

"Us, treason? We're doing that? Dan, you're all contradict-tions. I struggle just to get the paper out every day," says Bruton. "Fidel might not be too happy, either, right about now. Thousands of people seeking exile are jamming into the Peruvian embassy in Havana clamoring to leave the island. They also want trips, *out* of Cuba. Well, that's not my war."

"It's your war too, if you want this newspaper to survive," says Schuster. "And by the way, Harding is sleeping with that Cuban travel agent, the one in the photo. I'd say that's a conflict of interest even in Little Havana, wouldn't you?"

"How the hell do you know that, Dan?" Says Rosenfeld.

"I just know. Put your investigative team on it, Rosy. Check it out. Ciao."

Bruton and Rosy stand before the window looking at the newsroom activity. Then Bruton turns brusquely.

"He blames us for all of it, for Castro, for the Bay of Pigs, for the trips and for Rosales's death," says Bruton.

"Yes, and he's blameless. You've heard of shoot the messenger. This guy wants to shoot all the fucking messengers. Like the man said, Tom, it's bigger than that. It's all our fucking fault. We even started the fucking revolution. We forced those Cuban bastards playing dominos on Eighth Street to leave Havana. We should send them back again to storm their own fucking beaches."

"Would make a story. But we've got a helluva story right now, right here, Rosy, and we're missing it, man. It's sliding by us. You understand what that sonofabitch was really telling us, don't you? That we've been missing the goddamn story, Rosy. We're not covering the goddamn story."

"Maricones. What's that all about?"

"I want to see English translations on all of Harding's stories. Put the foreign and national staffs on this story and cover that funeral like flies on shit."

"Harding and El Jíbaro are covering."

"I don't give a damn. Double team it. I want a top English-language reporter covering and another photographer there. Treason, I'll show you treason, sonsofbitches."

"Hey Schuster, they didn't kill you yet?"

Daniel Schuster's eyes opened inside the womb on May 2, 1945. It was dark, then white with shooting particles of light. He was sixteen years old on the day he was born.

Slowly, his body gained feeling, and it burned up from his toes to his chest to his hands and his fingers, wriggling as the whiteness parted and the black face of an unimaginable being roared at him.

On the side of the snow-covered road to Tegernsee some kilometers away from the Dachau concentration camp, private first class of the 761st Tank Battalion, Gideon Jones of Harlem, New York City, passed his gloved hand over the nearly frozen face of a small boy, brushing away a seamless film of ice.

"He's alive," he yelled. The boy's eyelids trembled, and the eyes opened, and the boy's lips parted in a scream, but Jones only heard a soft, "Nein... nein." He slung the carbine over his shoulder and gently pulled the boy out of the snow.

"He's alive," he shouted, waving at the soldiers digging in the snow for bodies scattered by the final death march from Dachau. He carried the child, light as a sparrow, to a nearby field hospital. Gideon's unit continued south, checking the dotted line of frozen bodies for life. On his way back to Dachau, he stopped at the makeshift infirmary. A nurse told him that the boy in the body of a seven-year-old was really a teenager of sixteen and was doing well.

He found the boy in a spare dormitory tent sitting quietly on the edge of a cot, dressed neatly now in a baggy sweater and long Army fatigues rolled at the ankles.

Gideon parked his pack and M1 carbine in a corner and sat cross-legged on the ground, looking at the boy.

"Come here," he said, motioning, and pulled a Hershey's bar from his jacket. "Here. Take it. Good, good."

Daniel moved slowly toward him and grasped the chocolate, strangling it out of the foil.

"Hey, hey," Jones laughed at him. "Relax, Relax."

Gripping the chocolate, Daniel touched Jones's dark brown face with his other hand.

"Guess you never saw a colored man, did you?"

"Salivesalive," Daniel said.

"What you saying?" Jones said, and then he laughed. "You're alive, alive," he said. A nurse came in with a bowl of soup for the boy, and Gideon fell asleep. When he awoke, he found the boy on the floor next to him, holding his hand.

———

Daniel Schuster walked leisurely through the narrow streets of Kaunas, Lithuania, peering at the houses, and stopped in front of a small two-story building on Saula Gatve. The flimsy buildings on the street looked the same, he thought, but so much smaller, as though the street had lodged itself in a cubbyhole of history, hiding from his life in America, and had stayed stunted, tucked away for almost 40 years. He looked up at the windows of the rooms where he lived with his mother and father above their cobbler shop. A light flickered in the window, and it reminded him of the kerosene heater that warmed them on chilly evenings when it wasn't cold enough to fire up the coal stove. Kerosene, he thought, kerosene. And he imagined his mother sewing near the window, keeping an eye on the street.

He knocked on the door, remembering it perfectly, if from another perspective, in another color. He was nervous, perhaps because he had forced himself to forget in order to survive psychologically after the war. He smiled back at the woman who opened the door. Then he realized he couldn't remember any Lithuanian.

"I'm Daniel Schuster," he said in Polish. "This was my house before the war." He didn't know why, but he remembered some Polish, and she understood. The woman, a small, thin gray figure perhaps in her seventies let him enter and stood quietly, with a look of surprise, maybe chagrin, still clutching the open door as he stepped through the rooms. "I live in America," he said, understanding that the woman feared he was there to reclaim the property. The house had shrunk, but otherwise nothing changed, same kitchen, same bathroom.

He thanked the woman and left, not looking back, walking away from his old neighborhood, past the railroad station, restored after the Germans blew it up fleeing the Red Army, then along the Vilya River where he used to skip rocks. The smell was the same, a stink, and he stopped suddenly.

"Hey Schuster, they didn't kill you yet?"

It was Kasuk, one of the neighborhood boys yelling at him, running after him. He turned, but there was no one there, only the old terror and the stink of the lapping water. He wandered on looking for the site of Slobodka, the old Jewish ghetto where the Germans forced them to live during the first two years of the war. The Germans razed it too, and only a bronze plaque remained. He oriented himself focusing on the street and remembered that the Jewish police headquarters occupied the ground floor of his building, about a hundred yards from the ghetto's main gate.

———

His father called him the dummkopf because he didn't talk until he was four years old, and after that he never said much anyway. His mother would send him to Kushner's store to buy kerosene for the heater. Kushner would take the money and keep him waiting, standing in front of the high wood counter, seeing only the wood grain and the bottom lip of the empty kerosene can, forcing him to talk, to say kerosene. On the way back, he had to run past Kasuk and his gang, and they would always catch him and circle around him as he stood hugging the can of kerosene, his head down, not looking, imagining the kerosene can exploding, blowing the bullies up into the sky, beyond the train station into the river, then a shove out of nowhere would snap his head back, landing him on the side-walk, the can on the street with a thud.

Once, he left home munching on a hard cookie, swinging the empty kerosene can, and turning a corner he saw the gang running toward him. He ran, stumbled and choked on the cookie, a piece lodging in his windpipe, almost cutting off his air as he got to the store. Kushner looked at him, amused. Daniel banged the can on the counter. Only "aargh, aargh," came out of his mouth. "Kerosene, kerosene," Kushner said.

Help, help me, Daniel thought, but only "aargh, aargh" came out. Kushner laughed at him. Daniel fell to the floor. He was six by then and lying on the dusty boards next to a burlap bag of potatoes he realized he was dying, that only he could save himself. He stuck his hand in his mouth and turned pushing the hand in deeply with the weight of his body until he felt the thing and he pushed it aside and in a coughing fit spurted out the bite of cookie followed by flood of vomit.

When the Russians came in with riotous singing and dancing, Kasuk and his gang disappeared from the street, and the cobbler shop closed. Shop keeping was for capitalists, and soon, they said, there would be a factory in Kaunas making boots for the Red Army. The school was closed, and Daniel didn't mind. He was tired of the slaps he would get when it was his turn to read and he would look at the book and all the letters would jump and he tried to catch them but he couldn't. Now he spent his time with his father waiting in line for food coupons. Standing with his father and the other men, he imagined them boarding a train. That would be so fun. He loved the monstrous unstoppable efficiency of the machine, the imposing matte black cast iron and the flashing silver wheels whipping steel past Kaunas, and he knew that someday he would be on that monster heading away.

"We are socialists. We always have been. We are not religious," his father would say, but that didn't help them at all when the Russians found the hoard of leather in the back room, neatly stacked behind a shower curtain. His father was already in Siberia when the German Stukas bombed Kaunas and the Russians started to pull out.

Daniel remembered that day, the first day of bombing well. It wasn't so much the bombs that stuck in his mind, it was his question. For the first time, he challenged his mother. As they sat terrified waiting for each explosion, he told his mother, "Why can't we leave with the Russians? Now?"

"Go with the Russians, where? To Siberia with your father?" she said. "I can speak German," she said. "It will be better with the Germans. They're civilized people. Those Russian pigs — good riddance."

The Russians vanished and the neighborhood was quiet after the bombings. Nothing happened for days, then the dry goods store closed.

"Why no kerosene?" his mother said, and she dragged Daniel to the store only to find Kushner pulling down the shutter.

"Judith, you haven't heard?" Kushner said. He was a fat man and the folds of skin under his chin trembled as he talked.

"Partisans are taking the Jews. They take them from Slobodka over to the fort near the river and shoot them. They'll be here soon too." His fat chins trembled.

"Why are they shooting the Jews? We are Lithuanians too. We are not Russians," she said.

"They say we collaborated with the Russians."

"Everybody had to eat."

"Since when do they need reasons to kill Jews?" he said.

The Russian food coupons were worthless. Kushner would show up some days with canned goods and sipped some vodka with Judith. The roving bands of partisans, street toughs and criminals preyed on the Jews in Slobodka, but they hadn't come past the train station yet. The heater had no kerosene, so Daniel took it apart and cleaned each piece, looking for the source of the flame. He polished each piece and then fit them back together. He dripped the remaining drops of fuel into it and lit a match, watching the blue flames whip up and then fade and he imagined it twenty times its size warming the entire house, and he ordering it to start and stop like Aladdin's lamp in the story. He saw how it worked and sighed in satisfaction. His mother burst into the room and fell into the sofa moaning.

"Kushner said they're killing all the Jews in the streets," she said. "He said hundreds have been murdered at the fort. The bodies float on the river. Some are forced to dig graves outside of town and are shot right there. Where are the Germans?" She looked up at Daniel, "I should have listened to you. We should be in Russia."

Then a day later Kusak and the partisans knocked on their door. They burst in and dragged Daniel into the street, his mother's screams fading.

The partisans didn't kill Daniel, and he never knew why. Maybe the neighbor boys couldn't bring themselves to kill someone they knew. Maybe they just needed him to bury other Jews. But until the German columns marched into Kaunas, every night, the gang would bang on the door and drag him out. Every morning he was back, sometimes bruised, always shaking and pale with blood on his clothes.

"No, no. It's not my blood," he wailed at Judith. "It's the Jews, the Jews of Slobodka. We bury the bodies at night."

After the Germans came, the partisans faded away, and there was some peace. Judith spoke less and less and frequently sat all day long in front of the window. Kushner would show up now and then with the news. Edicts appeared from time to time in the newspaper. Jews must wear yellow stars, one on their left chest and another on the back of the left shoulder. The instructions were very precise. The stars had to be of a certain size and placed just so.

The star of David, he thought, and he decided they would be the finest stars on Saula Gatve. He cut the six-pointed stars out carefully, perfectly, and sewed them on each jacket with straight uniform stitches. Wondering how his father was faring in Siberia, he imagined him standing in a long line of gray uniforms, wearing red stars with jagged edges and only five points.

They were running out of savings, Judith said, but as it turned out, it didn't matter much. Three months after the Germans arrived, a notice appeared in the newspaper. Kushner brought it over with some leftover potatoes.

"We have to move to Slobodka," he said, slapping the newspaper.

"Why? I don't understand," Judith said. "Where do we live in Slobodka?"

"There's a lot of empty places in Slobodka now," Kushner said. "And anyway, they want us to leave our houses for the gentiles."

Later that week, the Schusters loaded a cart with a few belongings. When they arrived, the women and the men were questioned separately. Judith told them she was a seamstress, but they placed her on the clean-up crew that left the ghetto each morning to sweep the streets of Kaunas. Daniel said he was a shoemaker-apprentice to his father. His father had never trusted him to hammer a nail or sew a stitch, but shoveling snow in Siberia, he could never tell. At 13 years, Daniel started to look less boyish.

The rooms they found, above the police offices and the jail, looked down on the main street just a hundred yards or so from the ghetto's main gate. He could see the Jews march out in the morning to work in town, and sometimes they saw the gentile black-market peddlers stalking the other side of the barbed wire fence to trade food for gold. The Jews traded their remaining valuables, silver and gold, watches and furs, for food. Never a fair exchange, food was the only vital commodity in the ghetto and the risk was great. From time to time, the Jewish cops would catch a Jew near the fence, and Daniel would witness the punishment from the window. The sentence was fast and fierce. The cops shot the smugglers on the spot, then they kept the goods. Samuel, the head cop, acted as the judge and performed the execution. Dying was a way of life.

Drafted into the cleanup crew, Judith left every morning at dawn with the somber crowd of colorless overcoats that formed into a convoy of workers at the gate and marched off to sweep the gutters in the streets of Kaunas.

With Judith at work, Daniel foraged along the fence for anything dropped by passersby. It wasn't a bountiful harvest, but on occasion he found old razor blades. He sharpened them again by rubbing them back and forth inside an empty porcelain cup, then traded them for food. That's how his relationship with Samuel, the chief kapo, began. While he was searching near the fence, he felt a powerful force grab his jacket by the scruff and lift him in the air like a baby.

"Hey, have I got a smuggler here? Where's the contraband, you good-for-nothing!" Daniel wrestled himself to the ground, looked up to the towering policeman and pulled a rusty razor blade from his pocket.

"Aha! You know the punishment for smuggling rusty old razor blades?"

"Shooting me?"

"Yes," he said. "But we'll have to do it tomorrow. I'm busy today."

"Tomorrow?"

"Yes sir. Right here on the steps of the police station at 9 a.m. O.K.?"

"O.K."

"Make sure you show up, or the punishment will be more severe."

"Yes, sir."

The next day, he gave Samuel a shiny sharpened blade.

"O.K., sentence commuted," Samuel said.

"Is that worse than being shot?"

Each person was given 200 grams of bread per day and a few potatoes during the week. Daniel knew that couldn't keep them alive. It couldn't stop the hunger, only keep the body going enough to work and finally to die. Then he got a job offer.

Adina Nudelman lived a block away in a larger building of four apartments. He liked her golden hair and brown eyes, and he liked sitting on the front steps of her building telling stories. He would tell what happened at the gate, and she would tell who came to visit her father, the jeweler.

"I will be a shoemaker; everybody needs shoes, even the Germans," he told her.

"No, you will drive a train," Adina said.

"No, I will make a train, and I will make shoes too," he said.

"Make the shoes first," she said.

In the living room her father, an older man covered in a shawl, worked at a small bench. In a private arrangement with Samuel, the Jewish police would bring wedding bands and dental gold, the stuff they captured at the fence, and Nudelman shaped the metal into earrings and fancy broaches. Sometimes he would send Daniel, with the kapo's permission, outside the ghetto to the train station out to pick up the gold or make deliveries. Cohen the shoemaker, an old friend of his father, was one of Nudelman's sources. The Germans let Cohen keep his shop outside ghetto due to a shortage of shoemakers. Shoemaking had become a valued skill after the Jews were corralled into the ghetto and shoes traded for gold.

Then the call came for Nudelman to join the work crews, and the Jewish police couldn't overrule the Germans. "I won't survive that, Daniel. You go to the work gang for me," Nudelman said, "and I'll give you part of my bread ration." Daniel knew that more bread meant survival for them. He was only thirteen, but with a hat over his eyes, he could pass for an older teenager. Judith said it wasn't safe for him outside the ghetto, alone. Daniel listened then he said, "We should have gone with the Russians. Now I have to work too." He knew that what he said hurt his mother, and he was sorry about that, but it ended the discussion.

At least twice a week he went outside the ghetto gate to the cobbler's shop to deliver or pick up a package. He usually had about one hour after he finished with the street crew, before curfew. After curfew, the Jewish police arrested anybody they found on the street. On one delivery to Cohen's shop he watched the shoemaker sewing a last.

"Now they have machines that will do this. The machines will replace us. You'll see," Cohen said.

"What is that machine called?" Daniel said.

"It's called a niggerhead, a Jiminy Cricket niggerhead."

"Where is that machine?"

"The machine comes from a country called Brazil," Cohen said.

"Where is that country?"

"In America with Mickey Mouse and Donald Duck," Cohen said.

Daniel watched him sew up the shoe and later, on other nights, Cohen taught him how to hammer the nails on the last and punch holes in a perfect line and how to insert the heavy curved needle pulling the waxed red and yellow thread tight.

"You're good, you're good," Cohen said.

"I know how to stitch," Daniel said, "and I'm a good businessman, too. One day, in America I will have my own niggerhead."

One night he lingered too long watching and realized he was late for the curfew. The curfew, a routine part of his day had slipped by, a slip that could prove fatal. As he left the shop he heard a dark familiar voice. "Hey Schuster, they didn't kill you yet?"

Kusak chased him down the street, heading toward the train station, down by the river under the docks until out of breath Daniel slipped and found himself on his back, Kusak kicking his head and shoulders, leaning to choke him. As he twisted around to evade the boot, his hand found a rock and flailing at the air, the rock smashed into Kusak's nose knocking him to his knees. Daniel jumped to his feet swinging frantically at the bloody head until Kusak fell facedown into the gravel and lay motionless. "Kerosene, kerosene," Daniel screamed and ran.

He stepped into his building and raised his arms after the "halt!" and turned and felt better immediately when he recognized Samuel.

"Daniel, what the hell are you doing out this late?"

"Learning how to make boots."

"So, you know how to make boots now, eh?"

"I have boots for you, Samuel."

"Yeah? Where are these boots?"

"Well, in my head right now. I have to make them."

"Well tomorrow you can make them for me. Tonight, you are sleeping in jail."

"Why, Samuel? My house is right here, you know that."

"To teach you a lesson. You know, someone else, a German, would have shot you dead, and then what would Judith do?"

Daniel opened his mouth to argue but the conversation ended when a volley of shots and "halt! halt!" rang out at the ghetto fence near the main gate as two cops chased a man almost to the steps of the police station. Daniel stood by as they dragged the smuggler into the station.

"Don't move. I'm coming back for you," Samuel said.

Samuel didn't get his boots. The next day, when the Germans emptied part of the ghetto, Daniel was still in jail. He heard a commotion outside, and he stood on tiptoes to peer through a cloudy window and waved at his mother standing in line. She tightened the muffler around her throat and looked toward him without expression, only lifting one hand slightly and then they were ordered onto the bus.

Samuel explained that Judith had been moved to a work camp, and he would join her soon. In the meantime, he would work with the shoemakers. It didn't cross his mind until much later that Samuel had saved his life. Later that same day, Samuel came for Daniel and took him to the shoemakers. Three older men sat hammering over lasts.

"So, you were with Cohen," one of them said.

"Is he here?" Daniel asked.

"Cohen is dead," the man said. "Here, let me see you work this on the last."

The three cobblers examined his work, the kapo standing by.

"You're no cobbler," one of them said. Daniel looked at the floor. He knew that would doom him to the cleanup crew.

"Wait," the first cobbler said. "He can sew for me. I can make more shoes that way."

He went to work sewing for the three cobblers. But first, there was a rite of passage, they said. He had to join the guild, and they showed the tattoos on their chests.

"It's a special guild, Daniel," they laughed. "Very exclusive."

The purple pinpricks were applied with the cobbler needles and when the blood dried off, the numbers showed up neatly in an accountant's script. The number was scribed into the official rolls and on a document certifying his trade — shoemaker. That designation — 004711— carried him mostly unhurt through Europe on the train-cars west and finally to Dachau near Cologne where Samuel's protection kept him alive until the Americans found him on the death march out of Dachau.

Ashes to Ashes

Several hundred men, uniformed in camouflage, waving M-16s, react with shouts to Daniel Schuster, in battle dress, speaking from a makeshift platform in front of a huge bonfire in the Everglades. A gusting breeze blows drizzle on Harding and El Jíbaro as they fend off clouds of mosquitos. El Jíbaro's motorized Nikon spits and whirs as he pans the scene.

Schuster spots Harding in the crowd, pulls a .45 automatic from his holster and shoots at the sky. The crowd responds with a fusillade of rifle fire.

"What's his fucking problem? I thought he was a reasonable man."

"Nobody's reasonable when it comes to Cuba. They're always at war. It never ends. He's trying to repair his standing with the Brigade, what he lost with the dialogue. He doesn't like my writing, and I'm sure he knows I met Rosales in Guatemala. I'm always the fucking problem."

"He thinks you're involved in Rosales's death?"

"Who knows, I'm just a fucking impediment. Got enough shots? The photographer from downtown can cover the rest of it."

"Nah, he left already, trying to beat me to the darkroom."

The crowd releases another barrage of gunfire.

"Let's get the fuck outa here, man."

"No sign of a chopper."

"Forget the fucking chopper. Nano's just jacking off with that bullshit."

"Well, let's find the motorcycle."

They hustle along for about a mile in the rainy darkness until they come to a clearing where the cars are parked.

"No fucking motorcycle."

"And that's not all." El Jíbaro shines a flashlight on the flat tires of their car. "It's no accident. They got all four tires."

"Your pals did that."

"Wait, man. Looky here." El Jíbaro aims the flashlight at a camera bag forgotten in the rain on the ground behind the van. "They'll be back."

Headlights shine in the distance and a station wagon with two passengers drives up and stops alongside the camera bag. The car door opens and the driver reaches down for the bag. When he raises his head, he's looking at El Jíbaro's Smith & Wesson.

———

In the Little Havana newsroom, Nano speaks on the phone with the downtown newsroom in a sort of gargle as he stifles an urge to laugh. "Look Rosy, no. I don't know where the fuck Harding went. He called in his story, and you got El Jíbaro's film. I don't know where your guys are... all I know is that you got a story and you got the film. I didn't know Harding was corking the travel agent. I thought he was queer, always hanging out at Chévere's bar. Nah, I'm not going in there looking for him. Fuck you too, maricones."

———

Harding and El Jíbaro wolf down Laura's ropa vieja and plátanos maduros, steaming cups of café con leche. Laura brings more coffee.

"I'm sorry about stoming the paper this morning, Jonas. Nothing personal."

"Forgetaboutit. You didn't go to the service tonight."

"I'm not gonna celebrate the way of life that made him inhuman, that killed him."

"He was a cop under Batista, though. That way of life began back there."

"No. That was his foster brother. Manolo was in school, never into that until the CIA and the Bay of Pigs."

"You mean Schuster."

"Yes, Daniel Schuster — the Chevy man. He's on TV all the time. Both were orphans. A Jewish stepmother raised them both in Havana."

Laura walks over to the Brigada photo display and unpins the photo Harding had seen before, of Rosales in a group of young men in swimsuits. As she shows the picture to Harding, her finger starts on Rosales's face, then moves to Schuster. "That's Dan."

"Laura, may I borrow the photo? Jib, look at this. Can you blow it up for me, say twenty by twenty-four inches?"

"Sure. It'll be grainy as hell, though."

———

Harding and María park in the Art Deco district of South Beach, a rundown haven for retirees, mostly Jewish snowbirds from the northeast.

"Look at this, María."

He reaches over to the back seat and pulls out a huge photo enlargement of the group of young men. His finger traces over

Rosales's face, then moves over to Schuster.

"There's Rosales and that's his brother, Daniel Schuster, just released by Fidel after the Bay of Pigs." His finger moves down from Schuster's face to where a grainy number is tattooed on his chest. The number is partly blurred but the number 4711 stands out clearly. "There's your tattoo. Your man — number 4711.

"My god." She grabs the photo, shaking. "All those years chasing Rosales, and the guy was in Miami all the time. But why the number? Why a tattoo?"

"Come on. I want to you meet Uncle Frank."

They leave the car and cross the street to an Art Deco hotel. The sign says Snowbird. On the open porch, several elderly men and women sway in rockers, play cards. Uncle Frank, in a huge Hawaiian short-sleeved shirt and white Bermuda shorts, raises his hand to Harding. He's deeply tanned and wears thick trifocals.

"Uncle Frank. This is María Osorio.

"You finally got a girl. A real looker." Frank embraces María.

"A what?" says María.

"A looker, a looker, not a hooker. That means you're beautiful."

"Thanks, Uncle Frank."

Uncle Frank chortles, "More than that, you are *very* beautiful, blue eyes and blond hair, remind me of a girl I knew in Paris during the war. It's an old-fashioned expression, babe, and I'm an old-fashioned old man. Speaking of which, how about a drink. I make a *real* Old Fashioned, with the cherry. Now they say the maraschino cherry gives you cancer. That's crap. You can't make a real Old Fashioned without the cherry."

Harding holds up the print. "Another time, Uncle Frank. This is the picture I told you about. These are recently released Americans after the Bay of Pigs invasion in Cuba."

"Yes, I remember, what a disaster that was. Eisenhower and Kennedy." Uncle Frank peers at the huge photo, holding it in shaky hands. "Yes, yes. It's old. Jonas, you said he was from Kaunas. Could be from Kaunas, early in the war. Most Jews were just murdered at first so not too many got to this stage. Look at the ones and the seven, European digits."

"Kaunas," she says. "Yes, I know his family is from Kaunas."

"Yes. I interviewed Schuster after his dealership was fire-bombed and he gave some family history. He emigrated from there after the war, to Havana. That tattoo is most likely from a Nazi concentration camp where they held him outside Kaunas."

"Now I understand why Esther sent for him," María says.

"They want to forget," says Uncle Frank. "But that tattoo would be from the very beginning of the war. Usually there's two more numbers in front, I guess with time... Only a few like that made it all the way through the war. It wasn't until later in camps like Auschwitz where the Nazis systematized the numbers and the tattoos went to the arm. The Germans are fanatical about keeping records, even of their crimes. At the beginning, there was no system, and some were tattooed on the chest."

"I thought you'd like to know what that number meant."

"Gracias, Jonas." She wipes a tear.

"Oh, oh, when a woman looks at you with tears in her eyes, you are fucked." Uncle Frank takes her hand in both of his hands and shakes it lovingly. "Oh, you're a looker, Cubana. God, how I loved Havana in the old days, didn't you? It's the war, Jonas. It's always the same goddamn war."

María leans on the pay phone talking to Barrientos. Static pinpricks break into the call intermittently as it travels through a scrambler in Jamaica. "Where's Águila?"

"On sick leave. I'm in charge for now."

"What's wrong with Águila?

"Nothing serious. People aren't happy with the project. Things are getting out of hand here."

"I heard about the Peruvian Embassy."

"There's a thousand in there now hanging from the trees, and they're still coming. The whole country's on edge, waiting to see what we do. The diplomatic corps is going nuts."

"Get them out; send them to Peru. That's a fucking hell hole."

"You got it, María. Of course they don't want Peru, they want Miami. Fidel said to let the scum go, but it's more than a couple of thousand. We figure a hundred thousand are ready to leave and they're already bunching up in Mariel.

"Why now?"

"The exiles, the exiles from Miami. They have so much, and they spread it around and we're fucked by the embargo, still fighting a revolution just to feed the country. They're ready to trade dignity for a pair of Levis. We're stopping the visas, for now. The newspaper exposed the Havana connection anyway, and that basically kills the mission. Might as well close the offices."

"I'll close the offices, but the dam already burst... how the hell do you stop the flood?"

"Create more havoc in Miami. The exiles hate the paper. Maybe they'll blow it up. You can give them a little help. That'll send a message."

"Bomb the paper?"

"A little present from comrade Molotov."

"You guys are nuts. That won't stop anything in Miami or Havana."

"Terror has its own logic, María. You don't have to make sense of it.

María... María?"

"I'll close up here and come home, but no bombs. I'm not going there without a direct order from Águila."

"Look, they're so fucked up about the way the trips thing played out, I don't think you'll see Águila around here for a while."

"You pushed him out. You were working against him."

"If you want to look at it that way, O.K. I was never on board with this trips thing and now it's a total disaster. See you in Havana."

"Barrientos, convenient memory, fuck you."

———

I sense a change in María since the shootings in Núñez's church. Maybe it's the photo of Schuster and the visit with Uncle Frank. She's trying to process it all and for the first time, she seems at a loss.

I turn slowly to her. She holds my face and kisses me. Now I feel a different kind of fear, fear of losing her. And that fear rolls through my chest into my throat as I hear her voice rich with depth, and I thought of all the women I had loved and how each of them had torn shards from me and I in turn tore shards from them, the pieces fanning out like a myriad feathers pinned to a strange creature that was not a whole man but a bulletin board of scraps left by others.

"Open your eyes..." María says. "Jonas, strange, I do feel it's finished, but I'm not at peace, not satisfied. Is it finished?"

"No, it's not finished, and I'm not satisfied." I bring her wrist to my lips, and we look at each other directly, intensely. "Gabriela is still out there. The architect of the Salta Tigre massacre, the one who started it all, murdered Ramírez and his family, is still out there and means to kill me. I'm sure of that now."

María turns away as if unwilling to manage that thought. I kiss her face and her throat, her naked body, working down her scars.

"I'm going home," she says.

"Havana."

"Yes. Closing the shop here and going home. They want me back. There's a lot of unrest at home, and they blame the family reunification trips."

"What will you do?"

"Just disperse, as usual, but first, there's unfinished business here."

"Schuster?"

"No. I'll come back for him later, now that I know it's him. He's not going anywhere, easy to find. It's that Gabriela woman. She has to pay for Salta Tigre and if we don't do something she'll stalk you and send her assassins." Her determination frightened me, but I was attached to her, dovetailed into her, and there was no turning back.

Appointment in Coral Gables

The path was clear and simple for María Osorio. She had a mission, no other concern in life, and it was all-consuming. She called Barrientos, agreed to carry out the bombing strategy and gave him a list of the gear she needed to fulfill the assignment. "Just to start," she said. "I'll need more later." Her office in Havana found Gabriela's address. It was one of the big houses on Coral Way near the Miracle Mile shopping area, next door to Anastasio Somosa's mansion. The ousted Nicaraguan dictator was exiled in Paraguay, but his lover Dinorah Sampson, Miss Panama, lived there now. María told Harding he would help but that she would take care of the planning and the execution. First stop was the Flagship Bank on Miracle Mile. She retrieved the safe deposit box, found the usual purse, identical to the one she carried, and placed the contents on the table — a set of car keys taped to a note with an address on Southwest Eighth Street and ten thousand dollars in hundred-dollar bills. She placed her purse with the Mac-10, still unused, in the box and locked it away.

She waited two days, then drove the Mercedes west from her apartment on Eighth Street to a series of garages at the end of a strip mall near Schuster's Chevy dealership. One of the keys unlocked a garage revealing a white Coral Gables City van, and carefully nestled inside, a 10-feet-long belt of traffic spikes, one dismantled wood A-frame barricade, a surveyor's tape measure, a pick and a shovel, an AK-47 with three loaded clips, a 9mm Walther P5 German police pistol, a box of latex medical gloves and two hand grenades. The operation already carefully choreographed in her mind came together as she dryfired the weapons. The only things missing were two sets of overalls and baseball caps. She hadn't asked Havana for them, didn't want Barrientos to know there would be a second person involved. She'd get them at Sears. It was a lot of gear, but the preparation had to be complex to keep the operation simple.

The stakeout began with one day of training in the Everglades just off the Tamiami Trail. It was the entire script in slow motion, even the laying of the spike belt. Harding moved to help with the spikes, and she barked a "don't" at him. "Leave it. This thing can maim you." They fired the AK-47 and the pistol, not at targets — the action would be point blank — just to make sure they worked.

"I know how to handle a weapon," he told her.

"If it comes to that. But I hope it won't. If we plan it right there won't be any need."

Gabriela's house was well recessed, obscured by a thick hedgerow and connected by a long driveway to Coral Way, which runs at that point in front of the mansions, divided by a median and shaded by imposing Banyan trees. Each morning, three days before the attack, María parked on the median near the house, set up the barricade behind the van and nailed down Gabriela's routine — the black Caddy left the house each morning at 8:30 sharp. "The driver will die as well," she said.

After all the preparation, the action only took a few minutes. María lay the strip of spikes in the dark early morning at the head of the driveway, covering it with some grass cuttings. The Caddy nosed out of the garage on time and onto the spikes, exploding the front tires. The driver bolted out of the car but was caught by María's AK-47 as she stormed up to the open car door, fired into the rear seat and lobbed both grenades into the car. Harding packed the barricade and drove the van away glancing at the burning car in the rear-view mirror. He never fired the Walther.

"Did you see her back there?"

"The seat belt held her in and then the hedge jammed the back door."

Unfit for human habitation

María left two days later for Santo Domingo, connecting to Havana, without saying goodbye. "About us? Nobody loves like you, Jonas. For now, leave it alone. It's O.K." That's all she said after the action in Coral Gables.

The police and the media treated the assassination as a drug-related event, sparking a flood of speculation about the Guatemalan government's involvement in the cocaine trade, a stepping-stone north to Mexico.

———

The Avenida de las Américas sweeps wide and stately through Havana to the seawall Malecón like a gorgeous woman entering the opera hall with no escort. Few cars and buses motor through the boulevard of embassies and schools once lively as Havana's Champs-Elysees. Streets of century-old town houses feed the avenue. María found her apartment dusty but exactly as she left it. In the bottom drawer of her dresser she felt for the embroidered box Águila gave her with a small .22 caliber blue-black Colt revolver he had carried in a shirt pocket in the Sierra during the revolution. "You'll love it, virtually no recoil and sounds like a cap gun. But it'll kill." María loaded the revolver, five shots and an empty chamber to rest the hammer, then left her apartment on Calle 14 in Vedado and walked two blocks to Avenida de Las Américas and El Manicomio.

Using a back stairwell built as an escape hatch when the old school building was remodeled for El Manicomio, María climbed directly into the suite of rooms used for interrogations, connected to Águila's private office. Jorge Barrientos, an odd figure out of place at Águila's desk, looked up. A large poster of a dove landing on Fidel's shoulder as he gives his first victory speech has replaced Uncle Sam's bitter visage. In her mind, that said it all, the nuances of Águila's mastery of spycraft were gone with him. "Hola Sor María." Barrientos liked her nom de guerre and always greets her that way.

"Dónde esta Águila?"

"Sit down, María. I don't know. They arrested him here, and I haven't heard anything."

"Arrested? Jorge, what the hell is going on..." It was a demand, not a question.

"When people started storming the Peruvian Embassy, everything fell apart. We think that the hard time our economy is going through, food shortages and blackouts, contrasted badly with the exiles spending dollars right and left and drove people to rebel, to demand more. Now Fidel is opening the port of Mariel so anyone who wants to leave can just go. Did you close up everything? I didn't expect you here this soon. I thought you'd have more action in Miami."

"No, it just didn't make sense. Miami is already in turmoil and hundreds of boats are in Mariel picking up relatives. I guess that's better than just visiting relatives."

"Fidel is emptying some prisons to also send them some scum. They want you at headquarters to write up a report on everything that transpired here and in Miami from the moment the crazy preacher landed here."

"They already know. It was all approved. We didn't do it on our own."

"Not too many folks claiming credit. Right now, we're dealing with Mariel."

"I have unfinished business in Miami. I can't sit around writing reports."

"I heard you got Rosales. What else is going on?"

"It's personal."

"You can't go. It's over. I have instructions to place you under arrest if necessary and get that report written."

"Arrest? 'Tas loco." You're crazy.

"No. I have orders."

As she sat there before Barrientos, the heavy man leaning back in Águila's chair, a woman's tears for a man she loved wet her eyes, and as her hand feels in the bag on her lap for a tissue it brushes the beautiful little Colt, but they are quiet tears that just barely wet the lashes and in her mind four notes start to sound out slowly, slowly, do, re, mi, fa, separately and then together forming a chord, four clicks, four clicks, the single-action Colt's characteristic four clicks you wouldn't even notice unless you knew they lay in wait there, four clicks as you thumb back the hammer. Barrientos smiles, a benevolent smile at a woman's tears but only Águila sitting in that chair would know that the female form before him, head tilted slightly forward devotionally gripping the small straw purse, is not a woman but a thing he created from parts found left in the street like garbage, a hard thing of bone and gristle wound with copper wire tightly to the snapping point as the Colt plays out its chimes, do, re, mi, fa, hitting Barrientos's forehead with an almost soundless splat in the soundproof room, then two more in the chest without echo in the padded room and no echo in her heart, just her voice, do, re, mi, fa.

———

María left El Manicomio unseen through the back staircase and found Yitzhak Belman sitting on the stoop of her townhouse. "Hola chica. The neighbor told me you were back." He gave her an abrazo, and they walk up the stairs together. María tells him her work in Havana ended, and she intends to return to Miami. She has sublet the apartment, she said, and needs a place to stay for a few days. "Conmigo, claro." With me of course, said Yitzhak.

"I'll leave the VW with you and anything else you can use."

"I don't drive, but I'll take care of it for you. The house is a mess, though. The kitchen and the bathroom se cayeron, fell down."

"Se cayeron?" That was a new wrinkle in Yitzhak's old complaint. He always told the same old story, the one he says would make the corpse laugh at a funeral. Now pushing 70, Yitzhak still lives in the apartment he and his mother owned before the revolution. Near the harbor, the two-story structure was rocked off-kilter when the French freighter La Coubre loaded with 70 tons of munitions exploded in 1960 a year after Fidel took Havana. The event spawned a swarm of conspiracy theories, but no direct cause was ever determined. The fact remained, however, that Yitzhak's home was tilted, and the roof had slid to one side. In the new world of revolution, Fidel's government was there to help. Yitzhak went to the proper government office and asked for help to restore his apartment. The functionary was horrified and sent an inspector to assess the damage. Sure enough, the inspector said, this place was not fit for human habitation, and he filed a report. A year went by with no action so Yitzhak returned to the government office. Yes, the report was filed, but for an unknown reason no action was taken. A new inspection was required, the functionary said. And so on for 20 years. Nothing was ever repaired, and Yitzhak never gave up, returning to the office year after year. Unfit for human habitation, his apartment still stands tilted and crumbling, and he still lives in it. However, he told María, the last rainstorm opened a new fissure in the back wall, bringing a more troubling facet to the problem. One end of the upstairs hallway collapsed with the rain, and Yitzhak peered down at the scattered remains of his kitchen and bathroom. An inspector came by and declared the building unfit for human habitation. A day later two workers arrived and nailed a translucent tarp over the huge gap. That was a year ago, he said, but no work has been done.

"My God. How do you wash up?"

"Palanganas y el hueco en la pared." Bowls and down the breach in the wall.

"I have an idea for you Yitzhak," María said. "Since you don't drive, sell the VW and use the money to make the repairs. I'll leave a signed document giving you ownership of the car just in case you need it."

"Te voy a echar de menos, chica." I'll miss you, María, he said. Teary eyed, Yitzhak hugged her. "I feel like the day we found you." María hears that and pushes him away. "Found me?"

"Yes, at the end of the street, head resting on the corner marker, right on the Avenida."

"You found me?"

"Yes. I was visiting Esther and the boys. I took Danny and Manolo up the street to get a beer and there you were, a bloody mess, one bone sticking out of your chest. We thought you were dead. Danny leaned over and felt your pulse, you were a corpse but still breathing. He lifted you like a broken bird and the three of us carried you to the clinic, where the Colegio de Periodistas is now. You came to as we got there and scratched the hell out of Danny."

"No lo sabía. Nunca me dijo." I never knew, said María, Esther never said. She lost her breath and had to sit on the stoop.

"She thought you would feel bad if she brought it up."

"Yes. You don't know how bad," she said, head in her hands.

———

Ten thousand Cubans had gone over the walls of the Peruvian Embassy in Havana before Fidel deported them. By the time María decided to leave, two weeks later, Cuban exiles from Miami and Key West in hundreds of outboards, fishing boats and virtually anything with a motor that could float, were storming the port of Mariel, loading up with people from the mob at the piers and ferrying them to Florida. Most ended up in a sorting camp set up in Miami's Orange Bowl.

At the pier, María attached herself to a mother and daughter waiting for a relative to pick them up. María carried a small a bag that hung below her left shoulder under her arm, holding the Colt with two shots left and the hundred-dollar bills from the Flagship bank. The pistol was for protection as she crossed the Florida Straits from the escoria, scum Fidel had loaded onto the piers. When she made out the coastline, she let the gun drop into the water like a burial at sea. The money would help her resettle. Now that she knew the truth about Schuster, survival was her only mission. The need to find the real identity of her torturers had lost all meaning. They were the *them*, Batista's torturers, so many of them that only a revolution could settle scores, balance accounts, and it had.

"¿Qué eres," what do you do, the woman asked.

"Estudiante, medicina," student, medical school.

———

It's a Saturday and like all Saturday afternoons the Little Havana bureau is suffused with the aroma from Laura's caldo Gallego, a potent stew of white beans, chorizo and lard bubbling in a huge cazuela on a hot plate on the copydesk. Contreras's voice booms at Nano and Torquemada as he reads from a long ream of wire copy. "Thousands of Cubans gathering at the port of Mariel... Hundreds of small craft sailing to and from Key West and Miami and returning brimming with refugees. The U.S. isn't stopping them. The Cubans are loading the boats at Mariel and sending them back into the sea."

"Here they come, Mamita, sailing from an island of want to the land of plenty."

"Top story, thousands of Mariel Cubans are jamming into the Orange Bowl for processing into the U.S...." Harding says.

Nano freezes, then whirls facing Harding. "¡Coño tu madre! Jonas, how the hell are you, man? Where you been, I got used to you, man."

"Hiding in Miami Beach. See you're still feeding the monster."

"We got to feed the monster every day. What's a bald dwarf to do?"

"Nano, are we on the story?"

"We got the dregs. Downtown is all over it. We've got the hot Little Havana angle. Where you going?"

"Come on Nano. There's something you gotta see."

Harding leaves with a single wave of his hand at El Jíbaro and the other guys. Nano follows him strutting through the newsroom, rolling his shoulders like a samurai swordsman after the fight.

"Did you hear Núñez on the radio?" Harding says.

"Yeah. He says he was always working for the CIA, and everybody else was a Cuban spy, including you."

"I guess the religion of family reunification crapped out, so the asshole decided to change companies."

The wind buffets Harding and Nano standing high in the stands at the Orange Bowl looking down on the playing field, now converted into a tropical Ellis Island, as it opens to a never-ending stream of Cuban refugees.

"It's amazing when you see it like this," says Nano. "These people sacrificed everything to leave Cuba, but they really don't know what the hell they're getting into. It's a strange new land and a new language."

"And there's no going back."

"They have no past, no identities. They're born again."

"And there's no going back."

They gaze quietly at the seething activity below as the lines of refugees push slowly into the stadium. Made up mostly of ordinary families, the lines are peppered with bearded old men and outrageously tattooed toughs in prison uniforms.

In one line, María Osorio stands behind a small girl hanging from her mother's hand. As the line crawls forward, the girl trips and falls. María leans forward grasps the child's free hand and pulls her up again.

Epilogue

"About us? Nobody loves like you, Jonas. For now, leave it alone. It's O.K." With those words María Osorio disappeared from my life, dispersed as she liked to call it. It took me forty years to write the story of Salta Tigre and writing it brought her back to life. It's not journalism. It's just a story. Genocide in Guatemala has never stopped, but a weird preacher's crazy dream to open Cuba to family reunification became a permanent reality that was reaffirmed when Barack Obama's Air Force One jet touched down at José Martí Airport in Havana in 2016. Obama made it routine for anyone to visit the island. Shortly after Obama's trip, at seventy and retired from corporate life, I decided to visit Havana to connect again, even in a virtual way, with a woman I could never forget. Just like buying a ticket to New York, I flew to Miami and Havana, easy as pie. As I changed planes in Miami, I caught a glimpse of a newspaper rack, the headline in Spanish declared that American tourists were flocking to the island on scheduled airline flights. I had to smile, trips to Cuba in the news again, but I also felt the old loneliness, the orphan's solitude, wash over me like a tropical wave. They once said the Spanish language edition would not last five years. I decided to grab a later flight to Havana and rented a car. I parked near Biscayne Bay looking for the newspaper's stately glass palace but only a lonely cause-way marked the spot. In Little Havana, only the domino players were still at work in a cubbyhole stuck between two coffee shops in the old plaza. The newspaper, too, had dispersed. The pain cramping my throat wet my eyes. My body remembered better than I did.

I sat glued to the Southwest Airlines 737 window as we approached Havana, the green fields floating by and then a few leaning palms. Applause erupted as we hit the tarmac. From behind me, someone yelled out, "Hallelujah."

Acknowledgements

This is a work of fiction anchored in my experiences as a reporter and editor and thus I am indebted to nearly all the individuals who crossed my path during my work as a journalist. In particular:

My wife Zita Arocha, journalist and professor at the University of Texas at El Paso, for her constant support and belief that this story needed to be written, for introducing me to Cuba after we met in The Miami Herald newsroom in 1978, and for checking the manuscript for historical and cultural accuracy.

David Kaplan of El Paso, Texas, who survived a childhood in Nazi concentration camps, inspired me with his courage and humanity. I interviewed him over a period of four years and helped him write a memoir of that struggle, "I Forgive Them." To him I owe the details of time and place I used for the profile of Daniel Schuster.

Roger Fidler, journalism futurist who foresaw in the 1970s the advent and impact of digital journalism, world-class publication designer and dear friend since our early days at The Miami Herald, inspired me through his own writing to finish this novel.

Ileana Oroza, former Assistant Managing Editor at The Miami Herald and journalism lecturer at the University of Miami provided invaluable bilingual copy editing and made sure the Cuba references were correct.

 Lurene Noland, my high school English teacher who encouraged my writing, sending me into a lifelong career as a writer and editor and who delighted in spotting the flaws in this manuscript.

My family, a gang of freewheeling literati, approved of how I recalled our Costa Rican childhood and provided valuable feedback. My nephew Andrew Goetz proofread the manuscript and pulled me out of innumerable tight spots. My daughters Hilary and Miranda read through the manuscript and cleared it of slipshod moments invisible to the writer.

Thank you all, my beloved.

About the Author

David Smith-Soto, a bilingual writer, editor, journalist and photographer, taught multimedia journalism at the University of Texas at El Paso from 2004, retiring in 2016. Prior to his tenure at UTEP, he served as Managing Editor of The Winchester (Virginia) Evening Star, Editor of El Nuevo Dia of San Juan, Puerto Rico, Latin America Staff Writer at The Miami Herald and Managing Editor of El Miami Herald. He

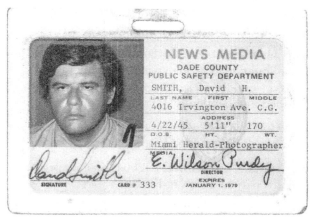

joined the Inter-American Development Bank in Washington, D.C. in 1985, serving as Chief of Publications and Associate Deputy for Public Relations, retiring in 2000. He earned a BA in English from the University of Maryland and an MFA in bilingual creative writing at UTEP. Much of his journalistic writing and art photography, including three major photography exhibits, is available online and Facebook. He lives with his wife, Zita, in Las Cruzes, New Mexico.

Publications

Havana Hallelujah: From Hardscrabble Reality to a Vision in a Dream, (2017) Huffington Post.

Havana Hallelujah II: Street photography captures grit and resolve after Trump slams the door, (2017) Huffington Post.

No Guns in My Classroom, (2015) Huffington Post.

A Liberal's Angst at the Dawn of Trump, (2016) Huffington Post.

You Can't Go Home Again: Article and photographs on the stream of undocumented immigrants returning to Mexico, (2007) Borderzine.com.

I Forgive Them by David Kaplan: A compilation of four years of interviews I taped with Mr. Kaplan, who survived a childhood in Nazi concentration camps, (2008) published independently.

Leaks: A short story, (2004) Rio Grande Review, the University of Texas at El Paso.

Maquila Maria: Opera libretto, (2004) first act produced at the University of Texas at El Paso.

Time Bomb Ticking: Award winning investigation that exposed the failings of the Virginia penal system, (1973) special supplement to the Winchester Evening Star.

A Study of the Virginia State Penitentiary: Following the success of Time Bomb Ticking, the Virginia State Crime Commission hired David Smith to investigate the prison and write this study. The scathing report was widely read in Virginia and led to some prison reform, (1974) book-length investigative report.

Photography exhibits

Havana Hallelujah — Cuban Street Photography: Exhibit of 27 color and black-and-white photos, some shot digitally and others on film, (2018) University of Texas at El Paso's Centennial Museum Photography.

Havana Hallelujah — From Hardscrabble Reality to a Vision in a Dream: A collection of 25 color and black-and-white photographs, (2017) David Anthony Fine Art (DAFA) in Taos, NM.

See with the Camera, Leave No Trace Behind: Exhibit of 25 photographs of 60 years of street photography, (2015) Glass Gallery of the University of Texas El Paso.

Footprints of the Borderland, Vol. II -- Border Senses: Exhibit of 20 portraits of Mexican farm workers, (2006) El Paso, Texas.

Made in the USA
Las Vegas, NV
23 August 2021

28725221R00134